MAGIC AND ROMANCE

A COLLECTION OF LESBIAN SHORT STORIES

NIAMH MURPHY

NIM PUBLISHING

For Louise...

IN RHYTHM

'One, two-three. One, two-three,' the rhythm went around and around in her head.

Kara clung to Felix as he led her this way and that. She focused on each move before it came. The heel turn, box step, into the lift... She tried to forget the pain in her feet. They were close to the end, it would soon be over, just a couple more moves. Then she could go home, have a bath, sink into the warm water...

"No, no, no, no, NO!" Kara and Felix jerked to a halt as their dance instructor, Ruby, yelled. She was a young woman, only twenty-five but already she had several trophies under her belt. She was tall, dark-haired and dark-eyed, beautiful, but intimidating. "Kara, are you even listening?" She had been giving them a tough time all evening, pushing them, over and over and over until Kara felt the music had no meaning left.

"We were in perfect time!" But Felix's protest made him sound like a whining toddler, not a grown man of twenty. He was acting the diva which usually annoyed

Kara, but today she was just glad his anger wasn't aimed at her.

"What does timing matter, if you two look like you're wandering around a supermarket?"

Kara stared at the floor. She knew she hadn't been feeling the music, she wasn't feeling anything right now. She was exhausted and just wanted to be done with this routine, done with this training session, and done with this competition.

Kara hated it when Ruby got angry. Not because Ruby was vicious or cruel; it was more because she hated to see her upset and hated to be the reason she was upset.

"You looked bored!" Felix tutted, infuriating Ruby further. "Both of you, but Kara, you just look like you want to be somewhere else entirely. There was no heart, no soul, no connection between you. You look like you are just going through the motions, and that will not impress the judges tomorrow."

Kara knew exactly what Ruby meant. But she didn't know what to say; she looked up at her and just felt stupid. Kara wasn't 'getting' this dance, they were dancing to a love song, and, although she got on with Felix, pretending to be in love with him was just weird. He was her first dance partner, and she was starting to think that maybe she should go back to dancing solo, or just quit entirely.

"Come here." Ruby held her arms open and Kara wondered why she wanted to suddenly hug her. "I won't bite."

Cautiously, Kara took a step forward and Ruby grabbed her hands and moved her into starting position. She was soft and warm and smelled so good. The thrill of being so close to Ruby sent a rush of excitement through her body that she wasn't quite prepared for. The sensation of Ruby's hand on the small of her back made the hairs on the back of her neck stand up. As she moved her own hand onto her teacher's waist, she had to remind herself to breathe.

But then she felt dread sink into her stomach as she realised she was going to have to dance with Ruby and dance well. There was so much spinning through her mind she wasn't even sure she could remember the steps.

But then the music started, and she had to move.

It was intense. Kara's heart was racing, her muscles were tight, and she felt herself stumbling through the moves. All she could think about was the heat from Ruby's body, the smell of her perfume.

She had to admit that in her most private fantasies she had thought about this moment. About what it would be like to dance with Ruby, to be this close and hold her instructor's body against her own. But now that it was happening she was numb, unable to think, and unable to move.

"Free yourself," Ruby whispered. "Forget about the moves, forget where you are, forget who you are, just feel it."

Ruby tried. She tried to let go of all her thoughts, all her worries about the competition, the analysis of the moves, the aching of her overworked muscles. She relaxed her grip on Ruby, relaxed into her, allowed herself to trust this woman, to trust her teacher, to be led by her, and then suddenly it just felt right.

She wasn't dancing, she was flying.

She was soaring around the room with Ruby. She didn't remember the steps, she knew them; they were part of the music and part of her. For those few brief moments, Kara was part of Ruby and Ruby was part of her, and both of them were a part of the music, moving as one across the room.

Then it was over.

Too soon it was over and they stopped, panting for breath. The exhilaration of the dance rushing through them, making them giddy with laughter. Ruby's eyes were bright, looking straight at Kara, and Kara knew she'd felt it, too, knew that Ruby must have felt the intensity burning through them.

"That was amazing," Ruby said.

Kara went to reply, to tell her she agreed; that it was wonderful, liberating, the most uplifting dance she had ever known, and that dancing with Ruby was the most powerful experience of her life.

"Well, if you could only dance like that all the time, we'd be alright." Felix had broken the moment. He grabbed Kara by the waist, giving her a friendly squeeze of delight. "You did awesome, kid," he said, grinning.

"Now see what you two can do."

Ruby was no longer looking at her, no longer smiling. It was back to business, back to coaching, and, as Felix took Kara into starting position, she felt like a cold, wet fish. All the life and all the music were gone.

Kara took hold of Felix's hand, she tried not to look at Ruby and tried not to think about how it had felt to dance with her. She had to think about Felix now; she had to focus on dancing with him.

Suddenly Felix was pulling her, the music had started, and she hadn't even noticed. She was two steps behind. Kara had to catch up, to jump ahead: she was back in the rhythm but she knew it wasn't neat. The dance was a mess already.

Kara pushed away thoughts about what Ruby might say, how disappointed she would be with her. She pushed away thoughts of the competition, the judges staring at Felix and her, the audience watching them, the other dancers laughing at them.

Worst of all would be failing in front of Ruby. Ruby watching her, disappointed, Ruby–

It was the lift. It was the lift already!

Kara hadn't been thinking, she hadn't been aware of where they were, she hadn't jumped, she hadn't given Felix the leverage he needed.

It was over so quickly.

One moment Kara's feet were in the air, and the next she was lying winded on the ground as Felix yelled out in frustration.

It took Kara a second to catch her breath. Ruby was at her side immediately.

"Are you alright?" Ruby asked. She placed her hand on Kara's shoulder: the intensity of the touch burned.

"Yes," Kara managed to say, "I think so."

"My ankle..." Felix said. The girls looked at him, he was pale and speaking through gritted teeth. "I twisted it as I went down."

Ruby rushed to him, leaving Kara's side, leaving behind the sensation of her hand on Kara's shoulder. But there were more important things to think about now. Felix had been hurt before, he usually took it well and Kara hadn't seen him in quite so much pain before.

As Ruby leaned down and lay a hand gently on his ankle, he had to stifle a cry.

"Okay," she said softly.

Kara could see she was concerned, there no emotion showing, she was completely poker-faced and that meant the worst.

"We'll get you checked out, just in case." Ruby forced a smile, but Kara and Felix knew what 'just in case' meant;

'just in case it was broken,' 'just in case it couldn't be danced on,' 'just in case this was the end of their ballroom championship campaign before it had even begun.'

Kara knew she should be worried about Felix, about how much pain he was in, and felt guilty that all she could think of was the competition, the dance, her career. It was her fault, it was her fault they had fallen; she hadn't been paying attention, she hadn't been focused on the dance, and now it was Felix who was struggling to climb up off the floor.

"Do you need a hand?" Kara stepped forward to offer her support to Ruby as she struggled to help Felix to his feet.

"You've done enough already," Felix snapped.

The words stung, they hurt all the more because they were true.

She didn't say any more to either of them.

Ruby helped Felix hobble out of the training room, while Kara watched, not sure what to do. She thought about waiting in the training room or heading home and forgetting about the whole thing. But she knew that running away would only make everything worse, so she gathered everyone's belongings and followed them out to the car.

The journey to the hospital was silent. No one had anything to say, and Kara knew they both blamed her. Felix and Ruby had put in so many hours, training her up to enter the competition, helping her to reach the level she needed to in order to compete with the highest grade of ballroom dancers, and now she had ruined it all.

She suppressed a choking sob and stared out of the window at the darkening horizon.

When they reached the hospital, rather than follow them into the doctor's office, Kara waited outside. She wasn't sure how long they would be, and she didn't know if she should wait for them or try to get home. Her body ached, her feet were sore, her muscles hurt, she was bruised where she had fallen, and it was all for nothing. Weeks of training, for nothing. There were less than twenty-four hours to go before the competition and Kara wasn't even sure if she would be ready, let alone Felix.

"Do you want a ride home?" Kara looked up to see Ruby.

"What's happened? Where's Felix?"

"He's waiting for his X-Ray results, but even if it isn't broken he won't be dancing tomorrow."

Kara had known that already, she had known and yet the confirmation was still devastating.

"I'm sorry, it's my fault," Ruby said. Kara was startled: Ruby shouldn't be apologising! "I shouldn't have pushed you both to dance again, you were way too tired, it was too much. It's just... you two are the first dancers I've trained, and I know you're both so good! You could walk that competition tomorrow. But now..."

"No, it was me! I should have been focusing more, I should have–"

"Felix tried to take the blame, too, but we all know who pushed for that final dance."

Kara stood up. She couldn't let Ruby take the blame for her fall, for ruining everything. "But–"

"No buts," Ruby said firmly. "There is no point, anyway. Blame doesn't solve anything. Now, it's getting late, shall I take you home?"

Kara nodded as her heart sank. Ruby was right, there was no point blaming anyone, it wouldn't change the fact that the competition really wasn't going to happen.

It was all over.

THEY SAID LITTLE TO ONE ANOTHER AS THEY DROVE across town to Kara's home.

It was a lot later than when she usually got home. But her parents knew she had been training, so no one had called. They would all think she was dancing, training, putting in extra practice, preparing for the big day. Kara knew they would all look at her with beaming faces as she walked through the door. They'd ask how training had gone, her mother would rush to fetch her something to eat, her father would tell her to get a good night's rest, her sister would want to hear all the news and try to make her put on her outfit again.

Then she would have to tell them, she would have to tell them it was all over. The competition wasn't going to happen: the support they had given her, and the money for training sessions, was all for nothing.

She couldn't enter the competition, she wouldn't get picked up by a talent scout or earn a scholarship. She'd have to start again, find another way to crack the industry.

She sighed in frustration, she was so angry with herself.

"How was Felix when you left him?" she asked, hoping to force her mind to think of other things.

"He really wanted you to get into the competition. He feels terrible for dropping you–"

"It wasn't his fault!" Kara insisted.

"I know. We can't keep going over it, we should just... I don't know." Ruby sounded tired.

Kara looked at her, even sad and upset she was quite beautiful. Her hands were firm on the steering wheel, she'd painted her nails red, ruby-red. Kara liked it when Ruby wore red, she looked good in it: she looked good in most things but she looked particularly good in red. She remembered how it had felt to have those hands on her, wrapped around her, delicate but strong, gentle but firm.

Kara looked away, she looked out at the road. She didn't want to have these thoughts about Ruby, not now, it was too confusing on top of everything else. But she didn't want to think about home, or about the competition. She didn't know what to think about. She wanted all the thoughts to just go away.

The car stopped. They'd reached her house. Kara sat looking up at her home. All the lights were on, they were waiting up for her, probably asking each other how much longer to give it before they called her. She didn't want to face them with the news.

"You can't sit there all night," Ruby said. It was meant to be a joke but neither of them laughed.

Kara turned to her; she looked at her in the semi-darkness and couldn't help but remember how it had felt to dance with her. She realised then that she never really wanted to dance with Felix, it was just a means to an end, just a way of getting into the championships. But she still wanted to enter, even without Felix, even if he couldn't come with her.

Kara knew that the moment she stepped out of the car the opportunity would be gone. Everything would be set in motion and she wouldn't be able to catch up. But right now, right now, she had one more chance.

"You could dance with me?" Kara said.

"What?"

"Tomorrow, you could dance."

Ruby looked taken aback; she stared at her for a moment and then shook her head.

"No, we haven't entered together! We haven't even

9

rehearsed! I mean this is so sudden I don't even know if I can–"

"The entry is in my name, it is me and a partner. Why not you?" The more Kara thought about it, the more it made sense. Why not? Why couldn't they? She'd seen loads of same-sex couples in the competitions, especially if they explained what happened to Felix.

"I'm probably too old for one thing–"

"You're not too old!"

"It's for under-twenty-ones."

"Only one entrant has to be under twenty-one, and you're only a couple of years older!"

"Well... look, I–I don't even have anything to wear."

"You must have loads of dance outfits!"

"None that would fit anymore..."

"Well, try them on tonight! Try them on, come tomorrow and we'll dance together and then the whole of the last few weeks won't have been for nothing!"

"What about Felix?"

"You said yourself he was upset I couldn't enter–at least now one of us will have a chance."

"I don't know..." Ruby looked worried and Kara knew not to push: no matter how badly she wanted it, she had to step back. "I really don't know, Kara, I'm going to have to think about this..."

"What's holding you back?"

Suddenly Ruby looked away. She turned and stared out of the window for a moment before finding the words to speak.

"I think you know..." she said quietly.

Kara didn't know. What could she mean? She couldn't mean...? Could she mean? "What do you mean?"

"I think you'd better get inside. It's late enough as it is."

"What about tomorrow?"

"I don't know Kara, I just... I don't know, okay?"

"Okay," Kara said. She knew she'd pushed too far, but she didn't quite know how. She backed out of the car and as soon as the door closed, Ruby was off. She drove away without a backwards glance. But those words were still burning on Kara's mind. 'I think you know...'

What? What did she know?

Kara didn't sleep well.

She kept thinking about Ruby; about them dancing together, about holding her and touching her.

When Kara had finally been consumed by sleep, she drifted into a deep dream; she was back in the training room, back with Ruby. They were dancing, their bodies held close and Kara wanted more; she wanted more of Ruby, she couldn't help it. Her hand slid down Ruby's back. Suddenly they weren't dancing anymore; they were somewhere else, there was no one there; it was just her and Ruby and the indulgence of desire and then she was awake.

She sat up in bed.

Torn out of her dream and ashamed of where it had taken her. She didn't want Ruby that way. Did she?

It was just nerves, it was just the dance, she was just upset, it was just the desire to dance with Ruby for the competition that had fuelled the dream.

But she knew that wasn't true.

The truth was that she did want Ruby and she couldn't lie to herself anymore.

Then suddenly, in a rush of understanding, she realised

that had been what Ruby meant when she'd said, 'I think you know.'

Ruby had known that Kara had a crush before Kara did. Ruby must have known how she felt, seen how she looked at her and that was why she didn't want to dance with her. She probably didn't even want to be in the same room as her. It probably repulsed her.

Kara groaned, embarrassed but unable to do anything about it. She was fed up with being alone with her thoughts and pulled herself out of bed. She didn't want to think anymore, it was all over anyway. Ruby would never dance with her, and Felix wasn't able to. So the championship was over before it had begun.

She traipsed downstairs, not bothering to get dressed or brush her teeth. She was just going to be a slob today, sit on the couch, watch TV, do nothing for the entire day, and maybe even for the rest of her life.

Her sister, Marie, was already up; sitting on the sofa with a bowl of cereal, watching cartoons, and texting.

Kara grabbed a mug of coffee and sat down next to her. As she did, she noticed her competition outfit, out on display, ready for her. A beautiful, sparkling, blue dress. She looked away. She wouldn't be wearing that today, she wouldn't ever be wearing it.

"Hey!" Marie said excitedly, as Kara sat down.

"Hey."

"What time do you have to leave? Are you going to put on your dress here, or take it with you?"

"I'm not going."

Marie's face dropped, she looked confused. "What do you mean? You have to go! Why aren't you going?"

"Felix has a twisted ankle, he won't be able to dance on it."

"I know, but last night you said your coach could dance with you–"

"She's not going to," Kara said sadly.

"She said that!?" Marie was incensed.

"Not in so many words, but–"

"Then what's the plan? Is there another competition?"

"There is no plan."

"You can't just give up!"

"Watch me."

"Kara, no! You have to go! It's all you've ever wanted! You used to say to me: 'find something you love and then find a way to make money from it'."

"I read that off a calendar."

"That doesn't make it any less true! Dancing is everything you are: you can't just give it up and go and work in a factory or an office or... or a chicken farm!"

"I can't go, I'd look stupid, I mean, she probably won't even turn up."

"Whatever you do, someone somewhere will think you're dumb for doing it, so you might as well do what you want because then at least you'll be happy."

Kara looked at her little sister as if for the first time. She was only fifteen, but just at that moment, she seemed like the wisest person she knew.

"You're pretty smart..."

"I just heard someone say that on a rerun of Cybill."

Kara laughed, she felt better for talking, but she still felt nervous about going. She looked at her dress. The thought of going made her stomach twist and turn with nerves, but the thought of not going, of staying home and never dancing again, filled her with a deep dread that made her jump up off the couch and run upstairs to get ready.

"He's sprained an ankle," she said, "so we had to switch around."

The registrar shook her head. "It's very unusual."

"But not against the rules," said Kara, hoping, praying, that she would be let through the doors into the changing rooms.

"No, not against the rules, but don't make a habit of switching partners." The woman signed against Kara's name and handed her the papers with her number on. "Locker room is second on the left."

Kara was delighted: she'd made it. But she still hadn't heard from Ruby, she didn't know whether she should text, or just wait, or maybe call.

The atmosphere in the changing rooms was buzzing. Girls were already dressed and putting on make-up; some, like her, had only just arrived and looked nervous. Many of the dancers seemed to know each other already and greeted one another enthusiastically. Kara wondered how sincere those greetings really were.

She found an empty space to get changed but kept glancing at her phone every few minutes, just in case she'd missed a text or call from Ruby.

Ten minutes went by.

Thirty minutes went by.

Kara sat, sadly, on the wooden bench; she was ready to go but still no Ruby.

The changing room slowly emptied as the dancers made their way to the green room; just a few latecomers stayed to finish their make-up.

Kara stared at the clock as it clicked over to a quarter to three.

It was too late.

Even if Ruby arrived this second, there was no way she could get changed in time.

Kara watched as the seconds ticked away on her only real chance of starting a dancing career.

The ten-minute call went out.

The last girl grabbed her water bottle and hurried out of the door. She gave Kara a confused look but said nothing.

Kara just sat, alone in the locker room, devastated.

She had known this would happen; she had been stupid to come. She had been stupid to believe that Ruby would just appear. She'd said she wouldn't dance, she'd made it clear, but Kara had wanted to believe she would just turn up and now she had made herself look like a complete idiot.

She started to pack away her stuff: if she left now, then she could sneak out without anyone spotting her. None of the other girls would notice she had gone, none of the judges would care; it was just one less person to look at. She could get a bus home, break the news to her family and just work something out later.

"I'm sorry I'm late."

Kara spun around to see Ruby, standing in the doorway.

She was wearing red, a sparkling, ruby-red dress that hugged her thighs. Her hair fell about her shoulders, her lips were red, her nails were red.

She looked stunning.

Kara stared at her, speechless.

"I had trouble finding this place," Ruby said. As if she had been expected all along, as if there had never been any question that she wouldn't appear. "I took a wrong turn and then when I got here that woman on the reception desk gave me the third degree. It's just a good thing I dressed before I left home... come on." She grabbed Kara's hand. "We'd better get a move on."

Ruby pulled her through the doors, and they headed towards the backstage area where all the other dancers were waiting for the call.

There were butterflies in Kara's stomach, spinning and fluttering in anticipation, but not because of the competition. It was the sensation of her hand touching Ruby's that made shivers of excitement run across her body.

Suddenly the numbers were being called. All the couples were filing out to walk the circuit of the ballroom in front of the judges, before the couples would dance, one by one. Ruby and Kara queued up with the others, waiting for their number: eight.

As they heard 'seven' Kara couldn't help looking up at Ruby. She wanted to see her look back, to see her smile, to see her excited to be there, to be dancing, competing. But her face was like stone, her jaw was set and she was looking straight ahead, concentrating hard.

Eight was called: they strode out into the huge arena. There were bright lights and, even though it was still early afternoon there were a lot of people cheering. Kara knew her family weren't there. She had told them they would make her too nervous to dance when really it was because she didn't want them to be disappointed when Ruby didn't arrive. But Ruby had arrived, she was there, and they were finishing their circuit of the room and coming to stand with the other dancers, while the final few were called.

Suddenly Kara felt like a real dancer: she was part of this competition, standing shoulder to shoulder with other, professional dancers who'd trained for years in ballroom dance. Just to stand next to them, to be judged on an equal standing with them was an achievement she had never expected to make.

Finally, they were all given the signal to head backstage again and wait their turn. It would be a long afternoon.

Kara stayed back for a moment, at the edge of the wings; she wanted to watch the first couple dance. They were good, but she knew she could dance better. She knew she had it in her to nail this competition and suddenly everything seemed to be within her grasp. Everything that had been so far away this morning was within reach.

Delighted at the thought of what she could achieve, Kara almost ran back to find Ruby, to tell her that the first couple was mediocre, their choreography was nothing compared to the dance Ruby had come up with.

But Kara stopped when she saw her. Ruby was beautiful: she was standing at the edge of the green room, a cup of water in her hand, and she was laughing as she talked to another dancer. A tall, good-looking guy, his chest almost bare in his opened shirt; his abs looked as though they had been chiselled from marble and, just briefly as they talked, his hand brushed Ruby's arm.

Those same words came flooding back into Kara's mind again: 'I think you know...'

It was no wonder she hadn't turned to look at her as they went out on the dance floor: she didn't even want to be here. Ruby didn't want to dance with Kara; the only reason she was here was to get a pupil through a competition.

Kara had almost managed to pretend to herself that Ruby was hers: for this afternoon at least, for this one dance, this one competition, Ruby was all hers.

Only she wasn't and she never would be.

Kara turned and ran.

She pushed her way through a crowd of dancers, ran down a corridor and slammed through a fire exit.

She stood outside in the alley, breathing hard; she felt sick.

There was a chill in the air but it felt good against her hot skin. She breathed in through her nose and out through her mouth. Trying to calm down and clear her mind, she didn't want Ruby to have this kind of effect on her.

She wanted to leave, she wanted to run away from the competition; the nerves were twisting inside her stomach and she felt as if she were about to throw up. The thought of dancing, of dancing with Ruby, of feeling Ruby's hands against her body when she knew Ruby didn't even want to be near her, made her want to get as far away as possible, as quickly as possible.

Except, right now, right this moment she felt too dizzy to even stand.

The fire exit door burst open.

"Kara!" Ruby called. "There you are, I thought I saw you come this way... Are you alright?!"

"I'm okay," she said, leaning against the wall, hoping Ruby would just leave her where she was, so she could just die in the alley.

"I'm terrified as well." Suddenly Ruby's hand was on her arm. She stood in front of Kara and took her hand.

The sensation of Ruby's touch relaxed her; she began to calm down as Ruby stroked the skin. Everything melted away and Kara just looked up into Ruby's eyes.

"This bit is hell," Ruby said, "but it will be amazing when it's over," and with that, she gently led Kara back inside.

Kara held onto her tightly, she didn't want to let her go; she didn't ever want to let her go.

They walked all the way back to the wings, ignoring the green room where all the other dancers had gathered to wait their turn. Instead, Kara and Ruby waited in the small space off-stage, where they could watch their competitors. Ruby occasionally commented on a move, or a dancer's positioning, but all Kara could think about was how close she was to Ruby, how it felt to hold her hand and how she knew that the moment they finished dancing together, she would never touch Ruby again, probably never even see her.

All too quickly their number was called.

Kara felt her stomach twist; the nerves about the dance finally kicking in. She didn't feel like her body was her own as she was led out onto the dance floor. Everything around them was in darkness as they took their place centre stage; illuminated by the spotlight, no sound, no world apart from each other.

"Free yourself," Ruby whispered.

Ruby's arms snaked around Kara's waist as they looked into one another's eyes and the music hit them like a wave, forcing their bodies to move.

Kara was flying, guided by nothing but the music and Ruby's hands upon her. It was as if she didn't exist at all; she was the music and there was nothing else.

But it was over before she knew. The world faded back into existence and Kara couldn't believe it had ended so quickly: she didn't remember dancing, she didn't even know if she had danced all the steps.

She stood panting, holding onto Ruby, who smiled at her then looked to the judges. But Kara didn't care about the judges; she just wanted Ruby to keep looking at her.

Kara didn't hear the scores, she didn't hear the audience cheer; all she could focus on was that Ruby had let her go.

She needed to leave. She had done what she came to do,

now she needed to go. She couldn't be around Ruby anymore, she couldn't look at her and want her and not have her. She couldn't.

Kara turned and left the dance floor. She hurried back to the locker room; she heard Ruby call out but ignored her.

Her bag was as she left it. She started grabbing her stuff: she wanted to get out as quickly as possible, go home dressed as she was. So what if she took the bus in her dance outfit?

"Kara! What are you doing?" Ruby had followed her into the locker room.

"I have to go."

"But you can't! We have to stay to the end, we have to wait for the awards–"

"I said I have to go." She felt hollow inside: she couldn't even look at Ruby.

Suddenly Ruby grabbed her shoulder and pulled her around.

"What's gotten into you?" Ruby looked at her. Her eyes were full of concern, her hand burned against Kara's bare shoulder.

"I have to go," Kara whispered, hardly able to say anything. "I really can't be around you..." She fought to say the words. "It's just too hard." She tried to pull away.

"Please don't leave," Ruby said.

Kara stopped. Her breath had been pulled from her chest.

"Sorry," Ruby said, letting go of her and stepping back; she looked shocked, surprised by her own words. "I'm sorry, I shouldn't have said that."

Kara looked at her. She didn't know what to say.

"You probably should go," Ruby said. "I've put us both

in an awkward position I just... I shouldn't have danced with you–"

"I'm glad you did," Kara said, sensing that this was it, this was the only time she was going to be able to say this, and if it wasn't now, then she would never say it. "Dancing with you, being with you, is... the most amazing experience I have ever had." Kara wanted to do something, to say more, but she was frozen, terrified by how Ruby would react.

"Kara, I..." Ruby looked away for a moment, then spoke softly and slowly. "I'm not sure if you really know what you're saying."

"I do know!" Kara said, suddenly desperate, suddenly needing Ruby to know how she felt. She couldn't be this close to telling her, only for everything to fall apart. "I do know! When we held one another, I knew for certain! It felt so right, everything was so right... and now I know I've messed everything up."

"You haven't messed anything up!"

"I have!" she said. "I messed up Felix's leg, I messed up the routine, and I messed up any chance we had of being... friends." She'd wanted to say something else, but the word had caught in her throat.

Ruby stepped closer. "You haven't messed anything up," she repeated softly. "Of course, we can be friends."

Kara thought about being friends with Ruby, about being close, but never close enough. About standing aside and watching her with men, men just like the one she'd been laughing with earlier. "I can't," she said eventually, opening up and finally admitting it out loud, "it's not enough."

Suddenly Ruby leaned forward and kissed her softly on the lips.

"Is that enough?" she whispered.

Kara was too shocked to say anything, she was in utter disbelief. She wondered if she was dreaming, if any of this was real; she wondered if Ruby was taunting her, teasing her about her crush. But the kiss was real and the way Ruby was looking at her told her that she wasn't mocking her.

"Why – why didn't you say anything?" Kara managed to stammer.

"I thought you knew. I thought it made you uncomfortable."

"But... I didn't know," Kara said.

Ruby smiled and pulled her closer. "You do now."

Kara couldn't hold back, not now, not now she knew she could have what she wanted. She grabbed Ruby, pulling her closer, kissing her deeply, hungrily. She wanted more and more of Ruby, and now she knew that Ruby wanted her.

"Whoa, sorry, guys!"

They broke apart suddenly.

Another dancer had charged into the room before stopping abruptly. "Judge's decision in five," she said and left quickly.

Kara couldn't help but laugh, the elation of being with Ruby making her giddy: she didn't care who saw them.

Ruby looked at her and smiled, taking her hand and Kara knew everything between them had changed.

"Let's face the music," Ruby said.

They walked briskly back to the dance floor, getting there just in time to hear their number called. They headed out to the arena together, it felt so different to the last time; Kara had been so excited to be there, so privileged, and now she just wanted it to be over so she could spend more time with Ruby.

The compère, an older man who looked well past any

dancing days he may have had, took to the stage and quietened the crowd. If anything, there seemed to be even more people in the audience now and Kara was surprised that so many people had turned out for the under-twenty-ones.

He started talking about the history of the competition and Kara had to force herself not to tap her feet in impatience: there were so many other things she could be doing right now.

He was about to announce third place. Kara looked up: if she had been placed anywhere, it would be third.

"And it is..." He paused, teasing the crowd.

'Come on,' thought Kara, 'this isn't X Factor!'

"Paul Robbins and his dance partner Sarah Gomez!"

The crowd dutifully cheered and Kara clapped along with them. She had seen the couple dancing while she had been waiting in the wings with Ruby... That seemed so long ago.

The compère was already prepping the crowd for second place. This time Kara knew she had no chance: the last couple had been good, this couple would have to be so much better.

"Fabio Cappelli and his dance partner Serena Fletcher!"

Suddenly Ruby gave a cheer, it surprised Kara but then she saw why. The dancer stepping forward was the same man she'd seen with Ruby earlier. Kara's heart stopped, and that moment came flooding back.

"He's my old partner," Ruby whispered.

'Of course,' Kara thought, shaking her head at her own stupidity and cheering along with everyone else.

Kara looked back at Ruby and wondered how long it would be before they would be alone together when they could really talk and get to know each other. She smiled at the thought.

"Kara Telfer and her dance partner Ruby Donovan!"

Kara looked at the compère. She was confused for a moment wondering why he was calling her. Did he know she wasn't paying attention?

Suddenly Ruby pulled her forward. "We won!" she said.

Kara couldn't believe it, she didn't even remember dancing: how could she have won?

She was handed a bunch of flowers and a gold envelope and looked at the crowd, stunned. Then she laughed. She had won!

She had danced better than anyone else and now she had qualified for other competitions, she would be able to get a scholarship, she might even be offered a dancing job. Her dream of being a dancer was becoming a reality. She was terrified.

She looked at Ruby: she couldn't have done it without her and reached out to take her hand.

With Ruby alongside her, then whatever happened next would be quite the greatest victory.

THE END

THE BLACK HOUND

I t was a dead place.

She stumbled as she navigated the awkward tufts of grass and gorse bushes, tripping as she caught her foot in a hole.

There were no paths or roads here, just a vast, open, unending space. No houses, no trees, no people, just the constant, biting wind and the occasional dried skeleton of a long-dead foal, abandoned in the hills and left to decay.

Isobel wrapped her shawl tighter around her shoulders. It was getting colder and darker as the sun, hidden behind its thick blanket of cloud, sank lower toward the horizon. She'd walked much further than she'd realised and needed to get back to the house before nightfall.

She came here to feel free, but it was an easy place to become lost, trapped in the wilderness, nothing but the darkness for company.

But that house felt like a prison to her. She had to get away and come out here if only for a few hours.

Isobel had arrived at Lansdowne just six months before.

It was a giant ruin of a house and the last of her family's

fortune. The memories she had of staying there as a child were happy ones, full of laughter and light. But when she'd arrived on that ice-cold October day she'd been struck by the forbidding darkness of the place.

She'd forgotten the great, black, iron gates, taller than two men and guarded by a huge stone wolf on either side, keeping their watch with distrustful menace. As the gates swung open to allow her carriage through, she had peered out of her window to gaze upon a shadowy replica of her childhood home.

All the charm that came with an ageing mansion had fallen away, leaving a decrepit shell. Ivy clawed along its crumbling walls, sinking its tendons into the building, and slowly tearing the stonework to delicate pieces that dropped from the wall, leaving gaping wounds in the house's façade. The windows, once thrown open to let light pour into the many rooms, had been sealed closed, blacked out from the inside with shutters, while the wooden frames slowly turned to rot. The grand front door, which had once been a bright, shining black, with gleaming brass fittings as polished and proud as a palace guard, now stood peeling and dull. As inviting as a cave.

The beautiful, mighty building of Isobel's youth had been infected with a disease, a disease that was causing its flesh to blacken and break.

That disease was Zillah.

Her uncle's widow, the Marquise, had appeared from nowhere and without introduction to the rest of the family. She'd married Isobel's uncle and taken up residence in his house, sucking up his fortune like a vampire. His health had deteriorated slowly, decaying like the house. Until he finally succumbed and left the family wealth and title to this mysterious, unknown woman.

With Isobel's parents cut out of her uncle's will they'd had nothing to leave her when they passed. She'd initially considered becoming a governess but then out of the blue, a letter had arrived from her new aunt, Zillah. It explained that as 'family' it was her duty to care for her niece and that she must come to live with her at once.

On that first day, the Marquise had swept into the grand, decaying entrance hall. She was a tall woman, slender and dark: she would have been extraordinary to look at in her youth and, as a woman of nearly fifty, she was striking enough to render Isobel speechless.

"So now I have everything my husband left me," she said with mild disdain. "A collapsing house, a landless title, and a penniless niece." As she spoke, she walked up to Isobel and took hold of her chin, carefully regarding the young woman's features.

"At least you aren't as ugly as the house," she said and stalked off without another word.

Over the next few weeks, she became more and more intrigued by the Marquise's decision to invite her to live at Lansdowne. They rarely spent any time together, and when they did, it was only so Zillah could watch, still and silent, while Isobel played the piano and sang.

No one ever came to the house. There were the servants, of course, Mrs Grantham, a caring but quiet cook, who preferred not to interact with her 'betters', and a gardener, Mr Harris, who was rarely seen and seemed to make little impact on the weeds, which were slowly consuming the house and gardens, burying them under an infestation of browning vines.

During those lonely months, Isobel had become filled with a longing despair that can only come from deep isolation.

Her respite finally came when Zillah hired a lady's maid, Kate.

She'd started at Lansdowne in January. After a bitterly cold winter and a dismal Christmas, Kate had been a fresh beacon of light and joy. Zillah was seen less and less, taking to her rooms sometimes a week at a time, and Kate would often be free to talk with Isobel. For the first time in months, she'd had someone to laugh and share her thoughts with.

But there were still long hours and sometimes days of loneliness when she wouldn't see a soul. It was then that she would escape to the moors, to walk along the desolate hills and spend hours wandering the countryside but never staying after dark.

Isobel picked up her pace. She wasn't usually one to hurry but there was something about this creeping night that made her blood run cold. She stopped to listen. She was sure she heard a howl.

She could see Lansdowne House up ahead. The gates were closed, and she prayed they weren't locked. The sun was sinking beneath the horizon. She had barely minutes before the world around her was plunged into night. As she came to the road leading to the house, she ran and was sure she could hear running behind her.

'Just an echo,' she told herself, but pushed herself to run faster, nonetheless.

She reached the gate and her heart surged with relief: it was open. She burst through and clanged the gate closed behind her. The clashing of the iron rang out in the darkness and she moved to pull the bolt across.

Something caught her eye, a shadow looming on the road. She thought it might be a silhouette cast by a tree or a rock. But something about it made her stop, made her blood freeze in her veins, her muscles tense, and her breath catch in her throat.

She tried to force herself to breathe, force herself to push the air from her chest, then lock the gate and go inside. But she was paralysed, staring into the gloom.

Then it moved.

The shadow moved towards her. She wanted to scream, to run, but all she could do was watch as it came closer. Stalking through the darkness, great black haunches, thick, black fur, and two shining eyes that stared straight into her soul.

They faced one another in the darkness. Just a few feet apart.

Isobel needed to lock the gate, she knew she had to lock the gate, she knew that beast could tear right through her. But all she could do was watch as the beast watched her.

Then it left. It turned and stalked off into the night.

Shaking, but finally breathing in hard, ragged gasps, Isobel locked the gate and backed away, before turning and running into the house.

She slammed the front door. The noise echoed around the cold, empty hallway. She locked and bolted it, hoping to keep as far away from that beast as she could manage.

"Will you be wanting your dinner now, ma'am?"

Isobel jumped at the sound of someone so close to her.

She turned to see the cook, Mrs Grantham, standing in the darkened hallway, but the cheerful smile on her face fell as she saw how terrified Isobel looked.

"Is there something wrong, ma'am?"

Isobel didn't know how to explain, how she could describe what she'd just seen.

"I..." she stammered, "I think I just saw a wolf..."

"A wolf?"

"Well, it was a dog, a black dog... but its eyes–"

"A HOUND!?" The woman seemed suddenly terrified.

"I believe so, yes," said Isobel, concerned by Mrs Grantham's sudden fear. "Have you ever seen one?"

"No!" said the woman. "I have never seen it, never. They say it is as large as a man, as black as coal, and with flaming eyes that look as if they know you."

"Yes!" Isobel was grateful that at least what she had seen was real and not some imagining brought about by the madness of isolation. "That's what I saw! Are they dangerous?"

"Dangerous?" Mrs Grantham looked at Isobel as if she were mad. "It is the Devil himself, ma'am, a portent of death, an omen! The house is cursed!"

She turned and hurried off back to the servants' quarters, leaving Isobel alone in the hallway.

She struggled to sleep that night. Her dreams were filled with black dogs and glowing eyes chasing her through the dark. She was fleeing across the moors, running faster and faster but it wasn't fast enough: the hound was gaining on her, its teeth bared, its eyes aflame. She could see the house but she couldn't reach it, couldn't get closer, and then she fell. The hound leapt upon her, all claws and teeth, ready to rip her to pieces. Only it was no longer the hound, it was the Marquise, Zillah, holding her down holding her tightly, ready to bite.

"Bella!"

She could hear Kate calling to her. She struggled against Zillah, struggled to get free.

And then she was awake.

"Bella, shh, you're alright."

Kate was there, holding her, stroking her hair. She

started to relax, to breathe again. She was safe: the dog was gone. Long gone.

"I'm sorry," she whispered.

"It's alright," Kate said, still holding her, "it was just a bad dream."

"How did you know?"

"I heard you call out."

"From upstairs?"

"I couldn't sleep, I was passing the door. But I ought to go: it's very late."

"Please stay." Isobel wasn't sure she could bear to be alone anymore.

Kate glanced at the door as if thinking that someone might burst through at any moment. Then she climbed in between the sheets, wrapping her arms tightly around Isobel who backed into her, feeling warm and safe; protected. As Kate leaned over and kissed her softly on the cheek, she felt a rush of happiness that she hadn't felt since being at Lansdowne.

"You shouldn't have to stay in this place," Kate whispered.

"I don't have anywhere else I can go," she said, and as she slowly gave into sleep, held tightly in the gentle arms of a beautiful girl, she decided she was happy where she was.

THE NEXT EVENING ISOBEL WAS SURPRISED TO SEE Zillah in the drawing-room, staring into the fire.

"Good evening, Aunt," she said, staying by the door, unsure if she should take a seat or wait for an invitation.

Zillah glanced across at her.

"I saw her last night." She spoke quietly, matter-offactly, but there was an air of threat in her voice.

"Saw who?" Isobel asked, unsure if there had been some visitor she hadn't been told of.

"Don't play with me, girl. I saw her go into your room last night and I saw her leave your room again this morning."

Isobel was horrified: she hadn't even realised that Zillah had been able to leave her bed, let alone stalk the halls.

"I had a nightmare. She came to comfort me."

"I'm sure she did," Zillah said. "I will not have that whore in my house any longer. She will be gone in the morning."

"What!?" Isobel was aghast. "You can't let her go–"

Zillah turned, enraged, strode across the room and grabbed Isobel's face with one hand.

"Make no mistake, child," she hissed, "you are mine. You are mine to look at, mine to watch over, and, if I so choose, you are mine to have. You are my possession and I will not have a servant girl taking to your bed."

Zillah pushed her back and Isobel stumbled. She turned and fled the room.

"Come back here, girl!" Zillah called, but Isobel had no intention of going back. She had to find Kate, had to tell her, had to stop her from leaving.

By the time Isobel found Kate in the servants' yard, she was so distressed by the violent encounter she could hardly speak.

Kate swept her up into an embrace.

"What on earth has happened?" she asked, holding her tightly.

"She says you have to leave."

"I know," Kate said slowly, "she told me an hour ago. I will travel in the morning."

"But you can't go!"

"I have no choice, Bella."

"But I don't know what I shall do if you're not here!" Her voice was becoming choked: she hadn't fully realised how much it meant to have Kate close to her.

"I'm sure you'll manage." She spoke cheerfully as if leaving was nothing, a mere trifle, and Isobel only felt more desperate to make her understand.

"I don't think I can face it!" she said. "I don't think I can face life without you."

Kate stared at her for a moment and wiped a tear from Isobel's cheek, smiling at her, a half-smile; a painful smile.

"I don't think I can face life without you either," she whispered. Then she leaned forward and kissed her, a soft, gentle kiss on the lips and Isobel took her in her arms. Holding her, kissing her back and pulling her closer, tighter, she couldn't let her go.

"So, this is where I find you."

Isobel pulled back to see Zillah standing at the kitchen door, a look of disgust on her face.

"In with the filth and the dogs." She marched forward and grabbed Isobel's arm.

"Let go!" Isobel shouted, twisting out of Zillah's grasp. The Marquise snarled and slapped her hard across the face with the back of her hand.

Isobel stumbled and fell to the ground, the shock rendering her motionless for a moment before the rage and fear washed over her. She scrambled up from the cobbled yard and ran.

She ran through the yard, to the front of the house and out of the open gates onto the moors.

She heard Kate calling after her, but didn't care. She wasn't going back to that house, she wasn't going back to that woman. She urged herself to run faster across the uneven ground. The sun was just setting but the moon was bright enough for her to see her way.

Suddenly Kate was upon her. "What are you doing?" she shouted, angry in her panic.

"I will not go back. I will not go back to that woman!"

"You have to go back, Bella, you're in danger out here." She glanced up at the full moon and then they looked across the horizon to see Zillah, silhouetted against the setting sun and heading towards them.

"RUN!" screamed Kate. Her voice was filled with panic, she looked at Isobel. "Run, get to the house, don't look back, RUN!"

She did as she was told, the fear in Kate's voice frightening her into obedience. She followed a different path, avoiding Zillah, but then she heard the wolf. The same blood-curdling howl she'd heard the night before: it was close. She sped up: they had to get back to the house, they had to outrun it.

Suddenly there was a scream, a high-pitched, gut-wrenching scream, a final scream. She turned, she couldn't see Kate. She had to go back, she had to find her, she could have fallen; it could be her screaming.

Then she saw it.

Standing on the peak of a hill, black as death, its bright, shining eyes turning to look at her.

There was nothing she could do. There was nothing she could do but turn and run. Isobel pelted across the moor, stumbling but not falling as she sped toward the gates of the house, clanging them closed behind her.

Then she stopped. If she bolted the gate, she locked them both out; she would be trapping Zillah and Kate on the moors with the hound.

She stared out into the darkness, desperate, hoping to see some sign of Kate.

But then she saw the hound, bounding towards her across the moorland.

She bolted the gate and ran to the house.

"BY DOGS, YOU SAY!" THE PLUMP, GREASY LAWYER eased himself back in his chair. "I had no idea."

"Wolves," Isobel corrected.

It had been over a month but she still felt numb. It was too hard to imagine and too difficult to think about.

"I didn't think we had such things." He shook his head and muttered as he chewed on his pipe. "She left you everything, of course."

"I understand," said Isobel, nodding slowly.

"All you have to do is sign the final terms, and the house is yours. Ah tea!" he said, turning as the door opened and the tea tray, laden with cakes, was brought in and set down on the table.

"Will that be all?"

Isobel looked up at her and smiled. There was just a small, fading scar marking her beautiful face, the only remnant of that night.

"These really are wonderful cakes, my compliments to the cook!" He looked at Kate, rubbing his sweaty hands together as he sat forward and reached for the largest cream pastry on the tray. "And, if I may be so bold," he said through mouthfuls, "what extraordinary eyes you have."

THE END

REASON TO STAY

I'd said: "No."

Now, I didn't have much time.

My chest was heaving, and my feet stung as I pounded along the street. I turned the corner and headed downhill; I had to keep going, I had to get there.

We'd only met four months before. We'd always lived in the same town but because we went to different schools, we never crossed paths, not until Georgie's seventeenth.

Georgie's okay. She's not a best friend, but she's quite a popular member of the group and she has been known to go a bit psycho. So, it's best to keep her onside if you know what I mean?

The party was epic.

Georgie's mum was blatantly overcompensating for being a single parent and the result this time was a massive house party, split over four floors and the garden. She seemed to have invited everyone; there was even a gang of oldies there, dancing away.

I sat out on the lawn, watching a bunch of Georgie's

drama group mates messing about. I think they were rehearsing for some Shakespeare thing, but they were just making the most of the opportunity to prat about in front of an audience.

That's when I saw her.

She had such confidence that she immediately stood out. One of the guys was a fencing champion, and she decided that her 'character' would madly tackle him with a tennis racket. He didn't stand a chance. I don't think Mercutio is meant to kill Tybalt, but there was nothing anyone could do to stop it. They were all too busy falling about in hysterics.

I was immediately drawn to her. I felt it deep in my chest. I ached. As if something was missing from me and she was the 'something'. She had always been missing but it was only now, as I noticed her for the first time, that I realised I could be complete.

I told myself it was because she was funny and fun to be around. I tried not to think about the fact that she had such deep brown eyes that you could get lost in. Or that her gorgeous smile was addictive and I wanted to do whatever I could to make it appear. I tried to convince myself that when she held hands with someone else and he gently stroked her long chestnut hair, it was the relationship I was jealous of, not his privileged access to the girl I had just become fixated on.

Because there is no way I could ever, possibly be interested in a girl. That just wouldn't happen.

I realise now, as I run, that I am completely crazy. I'm deeply, deeply insane and should be classified as 'mentally disturbed' by some git in a white coat, but, at the time, what I did seemed perfectly natural.

The day after the party, I waited at the end of the street where I knew the bus from her school would stop so that I could casually 'bump' into her and maybe walk her home. I sat on the wall outside the newsagents, where I could get a good view of the bus stop, 'revising' all afternoon for two weeks. I eventually stopped when it rained for so long that my notebook just turned to inky mush in my freezing cold hands.

Then I took to internet stalking.

I looked through all of Georgie's friends to see if I could find her. But I didn't know her name, and no one seemed to want to use their own face as a profile picture! Why? Why would they do this to me? I admit, my profile picture is a Llama in a hat, but that's beside the point.

I was devastated. Broken. Certain that I would never lay eyes upon this dream-like vision again! I went to my history exam completely unprepared and wrote a crazy essay on Henry VIII and how his madness and tyranny was driven by his passionate and unrequited love. Looking back, I'm not entirely sure I answered the question.

Everyone went to the park after the exam and as a group of us meandered over to our usual spot, we ran into Georgie. And Her!

"You've met Emma, right?" Georgie asked.

"Yeah," I said casually, giving her a slight nod just to seem all cool about it, even though inside I was screaming 'Sweet Hallelujah!'

I have no idea what kind of mental gymnastics I was pulling on myself to convince me that these intense feelings for a girl I had only seen from afar once were because I wanted to be her 'friend'. I am stupid beyond belief. Don't judge me.

But that afternoon; I was on fire.

What could have been better? The sun was shining, the park was beautiful, and I had an audience of friends all hanging on my every word. Then, to top off this glorious and magical afternoon, Emma and I got the bus home together! Glory of glories.

"You're quite funny," she said, and she smiled as she looked up at me. It made my stomach swirl and even the tips of my fingers seemed to buzz with excitement.

"Yeah," I said, carelessly, "I know."

"We should hang out more often."

"That would be cool," I replied casually, but I had to almost bite my lips to stop myself from screaming, 'YES! YES! YES!'

We swapped numbers, then I walked her all the way to her front door explaining that it was on my way home; which it was, if you were coming from the opposite direction, and we agreed to meet up at some point.

It took all my self-restraint not to send Emma a text or go to her house.

Ok, well I sent A text and, even though I walked up and down her street a couple of times a day from then on, it wasn't weird or crazy or stalking or anything.

Actually, come to think of it, she sent me a text first. Then I sent her one and then she sent me one and you get the idea. We hung out in the local park together and invited each other to parties until she became quite a regular in my little group.

One evening, Georgie went all 'loco crazy' at Emma and accused her of trying to steal all her friends. Emma left dramatically and, of course, I had the opportunity to go after her and 'see if she was ok'.

She didn't want to go home. So, even though it was late, we went and sat in the graveyard, the park being a bus ride away, and we talked. As it turned out she wasn't having such a great time because she'd broken up with her boyfriend (YES!) but all her friends had taken his side. Plus, her mum was ill and had to keep going to the hospital for tests and now Emma was messing up her exams because she was so stressed. So, I hugged her. It was the first time we'd actually touched; my heart was pounding so fast I was certain she would feel it. In fact, it was probably beating faster then than it is now and I've just run about two miles! But I can't stop running; it's 11:30, and the train goes at 11:47 and I have to make it.

Anyway, after that incident we became quite close. We started texting just before we went to sleep and first thing in the morning, and yes: throughout the day as well. We went to the graveyard a lot which sounds quite grim but it was actually a really nice place to sit, and on one really hot day we went down to the lake. She stripped down to her bikini and leapt in. I was a bit more reluctant; I had no idea what creatures of the deep were lurking in there, plus I really didn't want her to see me in a swimsuit, so I kept my shorts and t-shirt on, which was fine, until we got out and I had to sit in my soaking-wet clothes.

She held my hand.

I didn't say anything. It was like she was a wild animal and I didn't want to scare her off. I just stayed as still and as quiet as possible, while hoping that we could sit there, by the lake, holding hands forever.

"Thank you," she whispered.

I looked at her, I wasn't sure what she was thanking me for. She was staring out over the lake. A breeze coming off the water blew her hair back and the low evening sun cast a soft light on her face.

"What for?" I asked, trying to sound casual.

"Just... for being such an amazing friend and putting up with all my crap."

I grinned, stupidly. "No problem," I said, feeling awesome.

I don't feel quite so awesome now, right now I feel stupid. Really stupid. And I am probably all red-faced and sweaty because I've run so far. I should have got up earlier, or spoken to her before, or not been so stupid in the first place! Now I only have a few minutes left! I'm so close to the station, I can see it, I just don't know if I have the strength to make it in time. That is until I remember that night. When I remember that night, I can find the energy–I have to.

It was the night of the last exam. I'd finished my own exams a week or so before, but there was a maths exam that was officially the last exam of the year and so that was the night we had a big party.

It was down by the lake, there was a bonfire and a barbeque, loads of people had managed to bring along a bad mix of beer and vodka and everyone was there. Georgie was still being weird around Emma, and so were a lot of her old friends, which meant I got her mostly to myself. And I know how selfish that sounds. But I'm a horrible person.

It felt like Georgie's birthday party all over again, only better, because this time I was the one with my arms around Emma. I was the one who got to stroke her beautiful chestnut hair. I felt absolutely on top of the world because I had everything I wanted. At least I kept telling myself I had everything I wanted. But the reality was so utterly different... and that was why I made such a huge mistake. Not my first mistake either.

Emma was telling me about her mum's latest test and how the prognosis was good but they still had a while to wait on the results. I think by this point in the evening people were starting to whisper about how close Emma and I were, but we didn't care. Then I told her how strong she was and how I admired her courage and then... I told her how beautiful she was.

I couldn't help it; the words just fell out of my mouth. It was a combination of the firelight against her skin, her vulnerability and the four, five or six shots of vodka I'd had. But instead of being shocked or weirded out, she said: "You're far more beautiful than I am."

"I don't think so."

"You are! You're stunning, I've never seen anyone with such beautiful blue eyes, and you're so funny and kind and you're always there for me, and you've got such gorgeous lips, I just..." She touched my lips then, just softly, with her thumb as she held my cheek. I was a bit taken aback; I didn't know what to say. I knew that every second we were getting closer, and my heart was throbbing with anticipation but, stupidly, I didn't think things through. It just felt like the next step was to kiss her, so I did. I hadn't intended for it to be anything more than a brush of the lips, a friendly gesture, and although I wanted to kiss her more than anything I was still surprised by how much I wanted it. She pulled me in. Her hand moved to the back of my neck and held me there; I could have pulled away but there was not an ounce of me that wanted to.

I'd kissed boys before. Not many, as it happens, but still, I had experience. But to be honest, I'd always been bored; I hadn't really known why people were so bothered about the whole kissing thing and frankly, I was a little bit grossed out by it.

Until I kissed Emma. Until I felt like my whole body would burst under her touch, until I tasted her sweet, soft lips against my own. I bit her slightly, I couldn't help it, I was clumsy and passionate. More than passionate; it was animalistic. There was nothing in the world except her and me, and her lips against mine.

But then I heard them.

We weren't exactly hidden, and it hadn't taken long for everyone to see what we were up to, they shouted, cheered, laughed. And I stopped. I was devastated. I loved being the centre of attention, but not like this.

This wasn't what I wanted.

I couldn't handle it. I stared at them for a few seconds, dumbfounded, while a few people jeered and a couple of lads shouted at us to keep going.

I had to leave.

I struggled to stand up and stumbled away. I could still hear them laughing when I got back to the road. That was my first big mistake; leaving Emma to deal with a pack of teenage hyenas while I ran and hid.

I couldn't really believe what had happened. It wasn't until the next day that it really dawned on me that I'd kissed another girl. I started freaking out. It went something like this: 'I'm not gay. I don't want to be gay. Being gay is hard, too hard, too much hassle. And besides, I'm not. It's not like I fall for every single girl, it's just Emma. Emma is the problem, not me. She's just too beautiful, it's not normal. So, I just have to never see her again.'

I rationalised that if I never saw her again, then it would never be an issue for me again and I could get on and live my life not being gay. Genius.

"So, you were all over Emma last night." Why did I have to run into Georgie the next day? And why did she have to point out the blatantly obvious? Why couldn't everyone move on with their lives? It had all happened more than 12 hours before. Surely there was some new thing they could gossip about.

"Yeah well, you do stupid things when you're pissed." That was my second mistake.

"Is she a good kisser?"

"No." That was my third.

"Funny, Alice said she was." Who the hell is Alice?

"Alice?" I was trying to be 'nonchalant', I failed.

"Jealous much?"

"Shut up."

"Alice is the girl Emma cheated with, just before she broke up with her dick of a boyfriend. I thought you knew, what with you two being bestie friends now."

I didn't know about Alice. But I did know that Georgie was stirring.

"You really are a bitch, aren't you?" That was probably a mistake as well. Georgie is not the type of person who takes insults well, however, it hasn't come back on me yet, and I got the hell out of there before she could think of a reply.

My genius plan to deal with Emma, by ignoring her for the rest of our lives, had failed miserably by the end of the day. I got a text from her; she badly needed to see me. I didn't want to go. I really didn't want to go. I had a horrible feeling in the pit of my stomach that she was going to say she didn't want to see me anymore. Yes, I know I was planning never to see her again, but I knew I would never actually keep to that plan, so it doesn't count. But if she stopped seeing me... if she avoided seeing me; the thought of it split me into pieces. I felt sick.

But I went anyway.

"Sorry about last night." I spat out the apology quickly,

hoping to defuse any hostility, hoping she wouldn't blame me.

"My mum's got cancer."

All my little worries and thoughts seemed so stupid once she'd said that.

"I'm so sorry." I hugged her, and she cried. She cried for ages. I didn't say anything else. What can you say? Everything that came into my head seemed so stupid: 'it's not so bad' 'it's gonna be ok' 'everything's alright' 'don't worry'. See? Stupid. I just held her and once she calmed down a bit, she explained that her mum would have to go for chemo straight away and she would be ill for months. Then came the clincher:

"My aunt is coming to look after her, and my dad has said I should go to his for the rest of the summer."

"Don't you want to stay with your mum?" I was ignoring the fact that she would be away from me. That didn't come into it, now was not the time for me to be my usual selfish self.

"Of course, I do! But she says she doesn't want me to see her during chemo and it would make her feel better if she knew I was being looked after by my dad. Her actual words were; 'why should we both suffer?'"

"So..." I tried to process what she was telling me, I didn't know if her mum was brave or insane, "where does he live?" I thought I might be able to visit, go down for the day or a weekend, have a holiday, make it fun.

"Ohio."

"America?" She was going to America! For the whole summer! "When... when will you be back?" I tried to keep my tone calm and level, and completely not hysterical.

"That's the thing... I'm not sure."

"Two weeks? Three?" I was already back to being selfish.

"Well, if I'm there at the start of the school year, I might just... stay there. I have dual citizenship... and it's not like I'm exactly popular around here anymore... and my crappy AS results wouldn't matter so it would be a completely fresh start; it's actually a great opportunity...isn't it?" She was stammering and rambling and she wasn't looking at me.

I wanted to scream. I wanted to demand that she didn't go. I couldn't understand how she could leave her mother but, I also couldn't understand how she could leave me.

But what right did I have to stop her? I was just a crazy stalker. What right did I have to muck up her whole future? It was at that point, that moment, when she turned to look up at me, pleading with those deep, doe eyes of hers, that I knew I was in love with her.

"I mean," her voice cracked as she spoke, "it's not like I have a reason to stay, is it?"

'Your mum,' I thought, 'your school, your friends... me?' But I just said: "No."

That was my final mistake.

She started to cry again. I reached out to hold her hand, but she pulled it away.

"My dad's booked me a ticket for the 11:47 express to Heathrow on Saturday morning." She looked at me for a long moment and all I wanted was to tell her to stay. But I knew that I wasn't the person to say that. I knew begging her, pleading with her would only make her life more diffi-cult. I had to be unselfish. I had to let her go.

So I did nothing.

I watched her turn and go back into the house and I did nothing.

I did nothing the next day, and the day after that. Then the day after that; I did nothing.

I did absolutely nothing all week, right up until twenty-five minutes ago when I realised I only had half an hour before she was gone forever and I had been the dumbass that had told her to go. That's why I'm running into the station. It's okay; I have like, at least a minute, the train is only just pulling up to the platform.

I can see her, the wind is blowing her hair. It's such a cold summer's day that she's wearing a coat. She has a heavy rucksack and she lifts it over her shoulder, ready to step through the opening doors of the train.

She is going to leave.

I don't want to shout. There are too many people around; it will be mortifying. But if I don't she'll be gone.

"Emma!"

She stops one hand on the open doors. Looking up as I run over. I must look like a crazy person, but she actually smiles.

"You came!" She hugs me and I hug her back, but I have about three seconds before she has to get on the train because the whistle has just blown.

"I came to tell you..." I'm so out of breath I can hardly talk, "that you do have a reason to stay."

"I do?"

"Yes, absolutely, totally. I mean it," I look up at her and I know that now is not the time to protect myself, now is the time to be brave, as brave as she is, "I... I love you."

Emma looks at me, deadpan, for a moment and I start to wonder if I've just made another mistake. "I love you, too."

She doesn't get on the train.

Instead, she kisses me, right there on the platform in

front of everyone. Teenage boys, oldies, you name it. And this time, I don't care who sees us.

The train doors close. It pulls away from the platform and it doesn't take her away from me. She is in my arms and I have the chance to correct my mistakes,

"You're a great kisser," I say.

"And you're a great reason to stay."

THE END

THE KINGDOM IN A CAVE

E dris staggered on.
She pulled the reins of her horse, Arrow, forcing the reluctant beast to follow her through the thick mud that clawed at her boots, and the undergrowth that scratched at her face. Not for the first time, the horse suddenly tugged at the reins, spooked by something Edris could neither see nor hear.

"Come on!" she pleaded, but Arrow merely grunted, and Edris felt like giving up and falling to the ground, just letting the damp mud take her into its embrace.

Her muscles ached and her body was exhausted by the days of relentless travel. She felt certain her armour weighed twice as much as it did the day she'd left Mercia. The day she'd promised she would not return without success.

But that day felt like a lifetime away from the thorny weeds that stuck to her clothes, and the labyrinthine forest so thick with bracken and brambles that the sunlight could barely reach her exhausted frame.

For a moment, she thought of just letting Arrow go.

Letting him run back the way they travelled, go all the way home. He hadn't made any pledge, why should he suffer her fate? But the thought was fleeting. She couldn't make the journey without him. She didn't know what lay before her, but she had to give herself a fighting chance of getting home in time and for that, she would need a horse. She needed Arrow.

"Please?" she said again, this time barely more than a whisper, not expecting him to respond, but suddenly the tugging on the reins ceased. She looked up at her companion, and, although his eyes were filled with trepidation, she knew he trusted her, knew he would let her lead him on through the woods.

As Edris turned back to the brambles and continued to cut a path with her sword, she prayed she hadn't doomed them both.

Edris was risking her life, as well as the life of her trusting horse, on the good word of the people of Ardenford. It was only on their assurances that she had taken the old route to Northgales. It was a route no longer used, no longer walked upon, leading to a Kingdom that was no longer visited. A Kingdom that some said, no longer existed. A dark place shrouded in mystery and magic; but it was the place that held the last hope for Edris' people.

All shamans, fortune tellers, sorcerers, wizards, anyone with an ounce of magical knowledge, had agreed that the Queen of Northgales was the only one who knew how to help the people of Mercia, and Edris was the only one brave enough to make the journey to face her.

Slowly the path before her began to open out but as she struggled forward the weight upon her tired muscles seemed to grow even heavier. Edris fought to raise her sword to clear back the bracken, and she stumbled and struggled over the last few steps before making her way into a clearing. She fell to her knees. Exhausted but relieved, it had been hours since she had been faced with a clear path. She looked up hoping to see a cloudless sky above, but the dense forest canopy was thick and black. If anything, it was getting darker.

Edris tried to stand but her body was more drained than she thought. She felt even more exhausted now than she had ever been in her life. She dropped her sword, unable to hold the metal any longer, and fought the urge to close her eyes.

Arrow suddenly tugged on the reins.

"No," she said, weakly. But she turned to see him pull back, free to escape from whatever force was pushing down on her.

There was nothing she could do but watch as her horse escaped into the darkness. She knew then that Arrow had sensed the magic in the forest, had tried to pull her away, but she had ignored him and pulled them both into danger. She tried in vain to stand but instead, she fell back onto the soft earth.

Cursing her foolishness, she fell into a deep, dreamless sleep.

EDRIS AWOKE.

She was on a hard, stone floor but it was warm, almost hot. Instinctively she reached for her sword. It was gone.

She sat up, looking around frantically. She wasn't in the forest anymore and had no memory of how she had come to be in this place. The room was dimly lit but there was no torch or fire, no window or crevice through which the light from outside might reach her. Yet she could see.

Suddenly Edris realised the walls themselves were lighting the room. She reached out to touch the surface, it felt like normal stone, natural rock, yet it was emanating a soft green glow. She ran her fingers across the surface, it was smoother than she had ever known a mason to carve. It felt like a pebble as if the surface had been worn down with the soft running of water. There were no cracks, no edges where bricks lay against one another. The room was as if it had always been here, a perfectly sealed cavern.

The only way out was a wooden door, embedded into the wall. But there was no handle or grate and the edges of the door were behind the surface of the rock, she couldn't see a way to open it.

There was no escape.

Edris moved to the door. She had to try, even if it was locked she could pound upon it, demand to see her captors, let them know she was awake, let them know they'd imprisoned a servant of the King of Mercia and there would be consequences for defiance of such a king.

But as soon as she touched the door it was pulled open.

Standing in the entrance was a woman. A tall, beautiful woman with bright green eyes and hair as black as a raven's wing. She swept into the dungeon and loomed over Edris, regarding her for a moment.

"How came you to be in my Kingdom?" she asked, her voice sharp as a blade.

"I do not know," replied Edris, honestly, "I was searching for Northgales; my King has sent me on a quest to seek aid from Queen Ellawes. She is said to be the only one who can release my people from the pestilence—"

"So, you have come to demand a favour of me?" the woman asked.

With those words, Edris realised it was to the very Queen of Northgales that she spoke. She knelt before her and bowed her head, overjoyed that she was close to completing her mission, but knowing everything depended on the Queen agreeing to her request.

"I have," Edris said, "on behalf of my people, and my King. I ask that you bestow upon me the secret to cure and to bring forth life, so that I may save my people."

"You are mistaken," the Queen replied.

"But..." Edris was stunned, but kept her head low, "it is well known that you have this power."

The Queen regarded Edris for a moment longer before smiling.

"You are mistaken in believing that I will hand this power to you. I will not help you," the Queen reached out, forcing Edris' to look up at her with the gentlest touch of her fingers, "your King was right to have sent you, I would have killed any other knight who entered my realm, but you are fair enough to keep. You will stay here in my castle and serve me as you once served your King."

Edris stood, looking directly into the face of the Queen. For a moment, the briefest of moments, she felt tempted by the offer, tempted by the beauty of the woman that stood before her. But she knew this was just the magic of the Queen of Northgales, the magic to manipulate the minds of others. Edris was defiant; staying would be the coward's way out, to hide from the plague that devastated her family and friends. If her people were to be condemned, then she would die fighting to save them rather than scuttle under the skirts of a witch.

"My people are dying," she said, hoping that the Queen

would show some hint of compassion towards them, "if you will not help, then I must continue my quest and find another way to save them."

The Queen simply nodded before turning and sweeping out of the dungeon. As she went to leave, she looked back at Edris.

"Perhaps you will change your mind... given time." The Queen slammed the heavy door closed, and the sound reverberated around the cavern.

Edris rushed forward hoping in vain that it would somehow be open, that it would cave in under her touch, or throw itself open against her strength. But there was nothing she could do; Edris was sealed inside an airless tomb, left to die by the very woman she'd hoped would save them all.

EDRIS LAY ON THE GROUND, STARING UP AT THE ceiling.

She had spent hours banging on the door, calling out to whoever was beyond, threatening the guards, pleading with them, feigning illness. She'd charged at the door, hoping somehow, she would break through, but the wood was solid and after several attempts, she realised she would break her bones before she broke the iron clasps or the thick oak beams.

After giving up on the door she had inspected the walls, hoping to find a weakness, perhaps a loose rock, a place where she could begin to tunnel out. But the walls were smooth and rounded, there wasn't even a corner in this strange cavern.

Finally, through sheer exhaustion and thirst, Edris had

stopped. She lay down on the bare rock and began to sing softly to herself. Songs of home, the songs her mother used to sing and songs that she would sing with other knights around fires and in taverns, after victories and defeats and in the dark hours before a battle. She thought of home, of her friends, so many had succumbed to the pestilence, so many strong young men and women... Edris had known when she volunteered for the quest that she could die, that she would face dangers unlike any she had faced before, that she may end her life in the jaws of a beast, or on the sword of a bandit. But she had never imagined that her fate would take her to a slow and quiet end in a dimly lit cave.

Suddenly there was a rattling at the door.

Edris scrambled to sit up, she wouldn't let the Queen see her so defeated. But it was not the Queen Ellawes who entered, it was a young girl. She struggled through the heavy door carrying a wooden tray with a bowl and tankard, her hair was a soft light brown and hung loosely at her shoulders, her clothes were old and made of rough cloth which had been repaired many times; she lay the tray in front of Edris and, with a gentle curtsy turned, to go.

"No, wait!" said Edris, her throat so dry she was surprised she could still speak.

The girl turned back, her eyes were a deep, dark brown, and she reminded Edris of a frightened rabbit, caught in a trap.

"Stay with me," Edris asked, "while I eat?"

The girl hesitated, looking to the door and then back to Edris, before eventually pulling the heavy door closed, she then sat down on the ground.

"As you wish," she said.

"Thank you," Edris said, before draining the tankard, it was water, cool clear spring water and Edris was glad of it on her tongue. The bowl contained a green broth which tasted slightly salty and was surprisingly satisfying. Once she had eaten, the girl reached forward to take the tray, but Edris grasped her hand, preventing her from leaving.

"What's your name?" she asked.

"I mustn't stay any longer," the girl said, her eyes pleading.

"Just tell me your name and I shall let you go."

"Linnette," she whispered.

Edris smiled, it was an unusual but pretty name, "and you are a trusted servant of the Queen?" she prompted, hoping to find out as much as she could from the girl.

"I'm not a servant," she said with bitterness, Edris was surprised at her sudden change in tone, "I am a slave."

"Linnette," Edris whispered, seeing her opportunity, "you don't have to be a slave..." Edris didn't have a plan, but she couldn't let the opportunity slip through her fingers, "if you help me escape I will protect you, I will take you from here and you will be free."

"You cannot help me," Linnette replied, pulling her hand, trying to free her wrist from Edris' grasp.

Desperate, Edris pulled the girl closer.

"The longer I am trapped here, the more my people suffer," she whispered, "they are depending on me, people are dying, children are dying!"

"I can't—"

"You must!"

"Please," Linnette said, fear in her eyes, "you're hurting me."

Suddenly Edris looked down at their hands, hers were strong and healthy, holding tightly onto the thin delicate wrist of the young girl and at that moment, she didn't see a knight seeking support, she saw a tyrant commanding fear.

Edris let her go. Forcing this girl to do her bidding would make her no better than the Queen.

Unwilling to become that which she despised, Edris watched as Linnette cleared the tray and left the dungeon, taking all hope with her.

———

"The Queen has requested your presence." Linnette kept her eyes low as she spoke, unwilling to look at the knight.

Edris considered refusing, she didn't want to comply with even the simplest request from her captor. But she knew that it would be Linnette who had to go back and explain her refusal to the Queen and Edris didn't imagine the Queen would take the news well.

"Alright," she said, standing, heaving her body off the hard, stone floor. She was aching and stiff after a night spent in her cell, but she tried not to show her pain.

She followed Linnette out into the corridor and finally saw the castle in which she was being held. It was cooler in the corridor and there was a distant, soft smell of the sea, the walls were just as smooth as her dungeon, and emanated the same soft glow, there were no lamps or fires and no sound except their footsteps echoing around the walls.

They came to a stop outside an entrance similar to the one they had just left.

"Is the Queen in here?" asked Edris, perplexed.

"She wishes you to bathe and to change. I will come back to collect you," Linnette said, opening the door.

Edris was greeted with the sound of running water and the soft scent of water lilies. A pool, large enough to swim in was in the centre of the floor with rivulets of water running from the ceiling down into it. The pool gently overflowed into a small stream which ran into the wall and disappeared.

As soon as the door was closed behind her, Edris ran to the stream, thinking of escape, wondering if she could somehow get into the drains and find a way out. But the crevice into which the water drained was far too small, and she knew she would not be left alone long enough to widen it. Instead, she decided to do as she had been bidden and to bathe.

It was a relief on her aching frame to finally be rid of her armour and to sink into the hot water, but she didn't allow herself the chance to fully recuperate before she felt she ought to pull herself up out of the pool.

Edris noticed a long, thin, white dress which had been left for her to change into. She wondered if she ought to, as the Queen might be more willing to listen to her requests if she were a more compliant guest, but she dismissed the thought. She had no intention of bowing down to the Queen and so replaced her shirt, breeches and weighty armour.

"You are to wear the shift," Linnette said on her return, indicating the white dress carefully laid out on the rock.

"I know," Edris replied, "but I won't."

Linnette looked afraid for a moment, before turning, "this way," she said.

Edris was led up a long flight of stairs, through doors and along corridors. She began to realise that even if she had broken out of her dungeon, she could have been lost in this labyrinth of corridors for months before finding her escape. Everywhere they went, all the corridors and hall-ways, staircases and rooms held the same eerie glow, all were smooth in their construction and all were deeply silent.

"Where are all the other servants?" she asked.

"It is best you do not know."

Finally, the corridors began to change, the floors were covered in intricate patterns and the walls contained strange murals depicting wars and gods of a type Edris had never seen before. They stopped in front of a giant pair of gilded doors; the golden handles were shaped like beasts of the sea, with great gemstone eyes and scaled skin. Linnette opened the door and stepped back, allowing Edris to enter first.

Even in the King's palace, Edris had never witnessed a room as fine as the one she entered, it shone with the dazzling light of sparkling lamplight reflected a thousand times off mirrored walls, bright shimmering golden pillars, and a floor of pearlescent mosaic. There were gilded armchairs with plush, luxuriant deep red fabric, smooth as silk, covering deep comfortable-looking cushions, and hanging from the walls were intricate tapestries depicting scenes of dragons, sea monsters and a giant phoenix rising from a volcano. In the centre of the room, reaching up toward the high arched ceiling, were the four pillars of a giant bed, draped with cloths of red, with gold thread and blue silk threaded with silver, held back with a golden rope to reveal the bed itself, with a quilt of fine white silk, brightly embroidered with images of all the plants and animals of the sea.

Edris could not withhold a gasp as she stared at the luxury.

"Do you like it?"

Edris turned to see the Queen standing below a portrait of a great kraken tearing a ship apart.

"I have seen nothing to match it," Edris replied, trying to be honest without flattering her captor.

The Queen stepped over to Edris and gently ran a finger down her cheek. Edris was mesmerised by her emerald eyes as bright as gemstones. Ellawes smiled as Edris stared at her.

"It is yours if you wish," the Queen said softly, and Edris found she had forgotten why she'd ever resisted this woman.

"I can't..." Edris said but struggled to finish her thought.

"Wouldn't you like to stay in this room, rather than go back to that miserable dungeon?" The Queen spoke gently as she caressed Edris' cheek.

"Yes," she replied, unable to look away from the Queen's deep green eyes.

"Good," Ellawes smiled, "now why don't you make yourself more comfortable?"

Edris felt herself drawn to the bed, its comfort and luxury calling out to her tired muscles as she moved toward it.

"Why is the woman still armoured?"

Edris heard the harsh words, but it was as if they had been spoken through a heavy mist or fog, they were dimmed, but not silenced. She turned trying to focus on where they had come from.

"I'm sorry your majesty, she refused my instruction."

Edris could just about make out the curtsying figure of a girl, cowering before the Queen. She felt as though she should know her and yet she couldn't remember...

"Then you must learn to give better instruction," the Queen hissed.

As she spoke she reached forward, her hand had become claw-like, a bright green light, the same colour as her eyes, fizzled and cracked along her skin. Suddenly it burst from her, impaling the girl. Linnette's body twisted in pain and she let out a scream that echoed through the room and reverberated within Edris. In an instant, it cleared her mind, the fog vanished and she could see clearly what was happening.

"No!" she shouted, "stop!"

The Queen stopped and turned to face Edris, her bright eyes catching the knight off guard but she looked away and saw Linnette crumpled on the floor, shaking her head at Edris, warning her.

"You dare to command me? In my own Kingdom?"

She strode towards Edris, seeming to grow more menacing with every step and yet Edris knew she could not recoil, she could not allow herself to be intimidated, it went against everything she had ever strived for.

"I cannot let you torture her for my disobedience."

Her words did not abate the Queen's anger, she only grew more ferocious and Edris instinctively reached for her missing sword.

"You cannot allow me?" The Queen's hand reached forward, Edris saw the same light flicker across her skin and she knew what was about to follow. She looked up at the Queen, wanting to show defiance rather than fear, and at that moment the pain shot through her.

The air was knocked from her chest as every muscle in her body writhed, and her skin seared with the pain of a thousand white-hot flames. Edris knew nothing but the intensity of her body being ripped apart. Until suddenly it was over as swiftly as it had begun.

She lay on the cold mosaic floor, breathing heavily, it took her a few moments to remember where she was and what had happened to her. She tried to stand but fell back to the ground.

"I think," the Queen was saying as she left the room, "she needs a little more time."

Edris felt a gentle pull on her arm, as Linnette helped her onto her feet and guided her all the way back along the dimly lit corridors, toward the small, claustrophobic cavern.

Before she left, Linnette turned to Edris, regarding her for a moment.

"I have never seen anyone defy the Queen like that," she whispered, "you are the strongest knight I have ever known..."

Edris clutched her chest, it still rang from the sorcery the Witch-Queen had tormented her with, she was struggling to breathe, her muscles felt as if they had been torn from her bones and hastily thrown back again, and her head pounded as if it had been bombarded with rocks from every angle. She felt far from strong.

"I didn't have a choice," she whispered, her throat was dry and her voice strained, "some things are too important..."

Linnette was silent, she looked back down the corridor and then to Edris as if weighing up whether she should stay. "If I help you," she said, finally "will you promise me something?"

"Anything," said Edris, almost wishing Linnette would go so she could fall to the floor and try to sleep-away her pain.

"Will you set me free?"

"Of course!" Edris replied, surprised that the question had been weighing on the young girl's mind.

For the first time, Edris saw Linnette smile, there was a hope restored within her that altered her entire appearance; in an instant, she seemed younger, lighter, livelier and more beautiful. She nodded curtly at Edris, "when the castle sleeps," she said, "I will come for you," and with that she was gone, sealing the door behind her.

Edris lowered herself, carefully, to the ground, relieved that at last there was a way out of this godforsaken place, but troubled by the fact that her body may be too broken to take it.

———

EDRIS WAS SHAKEN AWAKE.

She couldn't tell if it was day or night, her body ached, and her throat was dry, but when she looked up to see the frightened, but determined, face of Linnette, Edris knew she couldn't let her down. She forced herself from the floor.

"Will the Queen come after us?" Edris asked softly, as they made their way along the same dark corridor as they had travelled just hours before.

"Not if we succeed," Linnette replied, but her answer did not fill Edris with optimism.

It crossed her mind that all this may be a ruse, a way of leading her into yet another trap. If she complied with the Queen, then she may be able to bargain her way out or escape when the Queen least expected it. Edris knew she was risking her life, and the lives of her people, on the trust of a stranger. She hesitated and Linnette turned.

"Are you unwell?" Linnette asked and placed a hand gently on Edris' arm, looking up at her with concern.

"No," Edris replied. In that instant, looking into the face of Linnette, she decided that if there was even the smallest chance this woman really did need her help then, as a knight of the realm, it was her duty to give it. No matter the risk. "Let's keep going."

Linnette led her even further into the darkness than before, the tunnels seemed to lead on and on, twisting and turning, plunging and climbing, yet never reaching anywhere. Edris couldn't tell if Linnette was leading her onwards or backwards, taunting her and teasing her with the idea of freedom but never showing her a way out of the dark labyrinthine tunnels.

"Where are we heading?" she asked, once she felt it was safe enough for them to keep talking.

"Deep in the castle," Linnette replied, "there is an Orb. It is kept hidden in the most sacred and least travelled part of the castle. I was once the Queen's... most favoured, so I know of this place well. I believe the Orb is the source of my tormentor's power. It contains the very magic you seek; the control over life and death. It is the only way out of this Kingdom of hers."

"Why have you not taken this Orb before?"

Linnette was quiet for a moment.

"I thought of it. I even touched it once, but the power of it..." she trailed off, "it was too much for me. I was weak then and I am even weaker now. But you!" Linnette stopped and looked up at Edris, her face lit by the soft green lights of the gently glowing cave walls, "You are strong, once I saw you defy her... I knew there was hope!"

Suddenly Edris doubted their mission. She had faced beasts and armies but had never fared well against magic. She wondered if Linnette's hope of freedom was clouding her good judgement or if they would get so far only to fail once they had freedom in their sights.

"How are we to take the Orb if it is so protected?" she asked.

"If we do not wake the castle, then we have hope," Linnette turned and continued along the corridor.

Filled with more unease than ever before, Edris quietly followed, wondering if they should turn back and worried that this quest had become too great a task for her to take on.

But, as she remembered the pain the Queen had inflicted upon her, she knew in her heart that she would not be the last to feel that power and this may be the only chance, however small, that anyone would ever get to stop the Queen, for good.

They slowly edged along and followed a narrow set of stairs upwards, it seemed to go on for hours and reach heights Edris didn't think possible, but eventually, they reached the top and came to an insignificant-looking door, barely more than a foot wide and just four feet high.

Linnette carefully pulled it open and peered through before she beckoned to Edris to look.

The room was bright, sparkling with the light of a thousand candles that hung in tightly packed rows on candelabras suspended from the ceiling. It took Edris a moment to realise that most were simply reflections in the bright mirrored walls, with pillars of gold separating each mirror as if it were a window, a window that forever looked back in on itself. Edris was reminded of the plush bed-chamber she had seen a few hours before, and rather than marvel at the splendour of the wall hangings and the plush furniture, she was sickened by it.

Linnette was pointing across the room, to a small plinth, on which sat a large open seashell. Inside the shell was a giant pearl, the size of a fist, gently glowing.

"The Orb!" exclaimed Edris, moving to squeeze through the door, but Linnette grabbed her and pulled her back.

Edris looked back at the Orb, and realised, with a deep dread, exactly why Linnette had stopped her.

Beside the plinth, on the huge plush bed, gently sleeping as if nothing could ever trouble her, was Queen Ellawes.

Hurriedly Edris closed the small door.

"You have brought us straight to her!" she hissed.

"It is the only time she is vulnerable," Linnette replied.

Edris looked down at her, her wide, deep brown eyes, were as innocent as a doe's. She wanted to believe Linnette, yet the danger they had been placed in filled her with dread. Edris thought of going back, back down the steep stairs, down the long corridors all the way toward her windowless cell, where she would wait for the inevitable fate that would befall her and doom her people. She couldn't do it.

But she thought of going through the door, the door that took her straight into the path of danger, straight into the bed-chamber of the woman who had inflicted upon Edris the most intense pain imaginable. She had crumbled under the power of the Witch-Queen and didn't think she could face it again.

Edris was caught between two unimaginable paths, she was afraid, but she knew that only one way gave her hope.

"What must I do?"

Linnette smiled with relief. "Just take the Orb," she whispered, "there is another door in the bed-chamber, one which leads out into the castle where we will make our way back out to the sunlight."

"The sunlight," said Edris, suddenly the thought of the sunlight on her face once more filled her with hope and joy she had forgotten existed.

"There is one thing you must know," Linnette's voice held a touch of darkness that immediately crushed the joy Edris had felt, "the Queen will hold the power of the Orb until it crosses the threshold of this Kingdom."

"What?!" Edris was stunned, the difficult had now become impossible.

"That is why I failed; the Orb needs to be touched by sunlight to break the spell. It is why the sunlight is banished here, but I know you will succeed. I know you will."

The faith Linnette put in her did not fill Edris with hope, instead, it filled her with deep guilt. There was a dread gnawing in her gut which made her certain she would fail, certain that the curses placed on her, her people, and Linnette were too heavy for her alone to lift.

She closed her eyes, trying to steady the beat of her pounding heart. When she opened them again, she looked deep into the eyes of Linnette.

"I will try," she whispered.

Suddenly Linnette reached forward and kissed her, gently on the lips. It took her by surprise and she found herself sinking into the softness of the kiss before Linnette pulled back.

"For luck," Linnette whispered. Then she gently opened the door to the bed-chamber and Edris knew it was time to face her fear.

The room was deathly still and quiet, the sound of Edris' boots upon the mosaic tiles of the floor seemed to echo a thousand times. She edged slowly toward the plinth, all the time aware of the Queen's gentle breathing, the soft rise and fall of her chest and the desire to stay and watch this beautiful woman sleep flitted across her mind. Edris turned to look at Linnette, she'd found the way out and was standing by a large open door which had been concealed by one of the mirrors, her face was pale, full of the same fear that Edris had felt.

Edris breathed deeply and turned to refocus on the Orb, less than an arm's length from the Queen. If she reached out she could grab it; if the Queen awoke she could have the Orb in her hand in just seconds.

Edris edged closer, with every step she was sure that the pounding of her heart and the shuffling of her feet would wake Ellawes. That their bid for escape would be over.

Edris could only marvel at the pearlescent beauty of the Orb, it shimmered and sparkled as if it were alive, alive with the souls of angels. She reached out her hand, wanting to seize it the second she could, she was just inches away. With a last gentle footstep, her fingers touched the pearlescent surface.

She gasped.

The surge of power shot through her with the ferocity of a thunderbolt, nearly knocking her off her feet. She stumbled, knocking the Orb from its plinth.

Linnette cried out.

But Edris caught the giant pearl just an inch from the ground. The pain from holding it shot through her arm, her muscles spasmed and she clenched her teeth to try to combat the sheer intensity of it.

"Put that back," hissed the Queen.

EDRIS LOOKED UP AT THE ELLAWES, AT THOSE beautiful, bright green eyes that filled her with dread.

Guilt washed over her. She was a thief, caught red-handed, the dreadful bounty in her hand. The Orb pulsated, sending a lightning strike up the length of her arm for every second she held it as if it knew it didn't belong to her, as if it knew its mistress was holding out her hand towards it.

"Put that back," the Queen repeated.

Edris knew the Queen still had her magic, she could cause enough pain to knock Edris from her feet and make her beg to go back to her cell. Yet she did not. The Queen stared at her and Edris felt mesmerised, drifting half-consciously toward the bed.

But then she stopped.

The pain in her arm was intense, and it seemed to anchor her to the ground. She knew she didn't want to go forward. She knew she wanted to go back. But she couldn't remember why. All she could see, all she could think about was those green eyes, staring at her, beckoning her. But she knew she shouldn't look. Knew there was something behind her she should see, should remember.

With all the strength she could muster, Edris held the Orb tighter in her hand, and pulled her gaze away from the Queen's, clearing her mind of the Witch's influence.

"Give me back the Orb!" the Queen shouted, enraged.

Edris looked behind her, Linnette was terrified, her back against the wall, too afraid to stay, but too afraid to run away. Edris knew what she had to do.

She held out the Orb.

"One move and I'll smash it," she said, making sure not to look the Queen directly in the eye.

"How dare you threaten me!"

But Edris wasn't interested in the Queen's rage, she backed away, toward the door, knowing escape was so close.

Suddenly Edris caught sight of something, glinting in the soft light of the Orb; her sword laying on a gilded table. Without a second thought, she reached forward and grabbed it, smiling at the sense of relief she felt to have her familiar weapon in her hand, before replacing it in its sheath and heading towards the door. Before she left, Edris glanced back and felt one last pang of guilt.

The Queen stood by her bed, beautiful in her nightgown, but fearsome in her rage and Edris wondered if perhaps things could ever have been different.

"You will not get out of this castle alive," she said.

But Edris didn't reply. She simply bowed her head in courtesy and closed the great mirrored door behind her.

"Let's go before she wakes any guards," she said, grabbing Linnette's hand and pulling her along a shimmering corridor.

"It's too late," Linnette replied.

Edris squeezed her hand. "It isn't, the castle still sleeps."

"No," Linnette said, pulling them to a halt, "once the Queen is awake, so is the castle."

"No, we have time—"

"You don't understand!" Linnette cried, "The castle is awake!"

Edris was about to counter her fear when she suddenly realised that the softly glowing walls around them were starting to move.

"Run!" she said, grabbing Linnette.

Edris didn't know which way to run, she had never seen this part of the castle before and as she ran the very walls moved and shifted around them. She held out the Orb in front, hoping that its light and power would somehow guide them through. But when she glanced behind them she saw the green shimmering walls were no longer walls, but more like living shadows, chasing them with the speed and certainty of a giant wave.

Linnette suddenly pulled Edris down a different corridor, their feet moving so quickly that they barely touched the ground. Edris could feel her heart pounding in her chest, her lungs gasping for more air, the relentless power of the Orb, but she knew if she stopped she would be swallowed by whatever it was that followed them.

Without warning Linnette pulled her left, into another corridor, this one darker, its walls black and then suddenly they were no longer in a corridor, but in a room, a giant ballroom. There were great tapestries draped from the stone walls and a dozen stone sculptures of giant beasts as large as two horses, with great sharp teeth and claws crouched on plinths all around the room and bathed in the light of candles.

Edris turned to look at the door and, as she suspected, saw the strange shadows gathered at the doorway but not moving into the room, unable to journey into the candlelight.

She stopped. Breathing heavily.

"We must keep going!" cried Linnette, panting as hard as Edris.

"They can't follow us here," Edris said, pointing back to the softly glowing shadows.

"I know, but—" she stopped, her eye caught on something behind Edris' shoulder.

Edris turned, expecting to see the shadows, there was nothing but sculptures and tapestries. Linnette tugged her arm.

"We have to go," she whispered, the fear tainting on her voice.

Edris looked around again, the walls were still, nothing new had entered the well-lit room.

But then, Edris realised with deep horror, their relentless escape was far from over. The stone beasts were coming to life.

———

It felt as if the very earth beneath their feet

was moving as the deafening sound of rock grating against rock filled the room. The great stone beasts turned their giant heads in unison, staring down at Edris and Linnette with bright emerald eyes.

Edris hardly had the breath to scream, so terrifying was the spectacle before her. She moved backwards slowly, hoping that her careful movements wouldn't rouse the beasts' attention, but as she did so Linnette gently tugged her arm and Edris turned to see another beast behind them, and another to the left, and another, and another. They were surrounded.

Edris drew her sword, knowing that her blade would be useless against flesh carved from rock, but she had nothing else to defend them with. She clenched her teeth as the Orb began to pulsate once again as if sensing her fear and feeding off it.

"Which way?" Edris hissed.

"They are all around us!" Linnette replied, the panic clear in her voice.

"But which way is out?" Edris asked. If they were going to make a run for it then she wanted to make sure they would be running in the right direction.

"That door." Linnette pointed to an archway leading down a brightly lit corridor with the similar mosaic tiles and mirrored walls. There were at least three beasts between them and their exit. But Edris was thankful that at least she did not have to go back into the way of those glimmering shadows.

Edris felt Linnette squeeze her arm as the beasts closed in on them, slowly, as if wanting to make a feast of their fear before finishing them off.

Suddenly one of them swiped a sharp, clawed paw in their direction, Edris leapt back, away from the swipe, and instinctively she raised her sword. She screamed as the power of the Orb shot through her. But her scream was drowned out by the sound of sword crashing against stone so hard that the rock shattered before them. Edris was sent flying across the room, where she hit the wall and slid to the ground, still clutching the Orb.

The beast howled a dreadful, unearthly howl of anguish and the other beasts backed away from the strange knight who wielded such power.

Linnette ran to Edris and struggled to help her off the floor.

"You can defeat them!" she cried.

"I don't know if I can do that again," Edris replied, as she struggled to stand, her body felt battered and broken, the Orb still pulsated in her hand and although she felt certain that the power of the Orb would enable her to fight the beasts, she wasn't sure she could survive another blow.

"Come on," said Linnette, unwilling to test her words.

The beasts paced as they watched the two women edge towards the door, Edris still clutching her sword. Then one of them, a carved gryphon, charged. Edris held her breath and steadied herself. As the beast crashed forward she struck out, catching the beast's giant, open jaw mid-pounce. Its face shattered, sending a thousand pieces of rock and stone hurtling in every direction and knocking them both off their feet.

Edris' sword arm was numb. She desperately scrambled from the floor, checking around for Linnette, who looked frightened but unhurt.

"Run," she said.

Linnette didn't have to be asked twice, she was on her feet and pelting down the corridor before Edris even had a chance to stand. But she followed as quickly as she could.

She turned back to look at the beasts, they were hesitant, unwilling to move. For a moment, she thought she might be safe, but then, as if all at once they had the same urge, the beasts began to give chase.

She turned and followed Linnette, running as fast as she could manage. All she could hear was the sound of stone cracking against rock as the great beasts pursued them.

Linnette turned along one corridor, then just as quick down another. Going left and right and zigzagging through the castle. The confusion slowed the beasts, but it didn't stop them.

Edris didn't have a chance to marvel at the beauty and majesty of the castle; the way the light sparkled off the walls and glimmered on the marble floors. The constant hammering of dozens of stone feet ensured she didn't pause as she ran out of the castle doors and into a great open court-yard. She didn't have a chance to stand and stare at the luxurious gardens, with thousands of strange but colourful plants and flowing waterfalls, all under a ceiling of rock, buried deep beneath the earth; a kingdom in a cave.

With no more corridors to turn down and confuse the beasts, Edris and Linnette were easy targets. The beasts came crashing through the grand entrance hall and pounded through the great gardens. They were catching up.

But Linnette continued to run, and Edris followed, desperately hoping she knew where she was taking them. They ran along a gravel path between two tall hedgerows of glimmering stalagmites, and suddenly Linnette turned off the path and down a mossy bank. Edris gasped as she saw what was before them. A huge, black lake, surrounding them as far as the eye could see.

Edris paused.

The beasts were gaining, she had to trust Linnette. She followed her down the mossy bank and toward a small wooden jetty. There were several rowing boats moored and Linnette was struggling to untie one.

With a swift slice of her sword, the rope was cut, and the boat was free but Edris had little idea what they were going to be rowing towards. Before them, out of the light of the castle, was blackness.

Linnette took the oars and Edris hopped into the boat after her, readying herself for the beasts who were charging down the bank after them.

Once again, the beasts hesitated at the edge of the water. Unwilling to enter the black depths, but their eyes flashed with the bright emerald green light of the Witch-Queen and almost immediately one leapt into the water. But its heavy stone frame prevented it from swimming, and it immediately disappeared.

Edris almost laughed with relief.

But her relief was short-lived.

A second then a third beast took a running jump into the water and with its great stone paw, one of the beasts caught the edge of the boat, it's claws ripping the wood as if it was nothing more than silk.

Linnette cried out as the boat rocked ferociously, they managed to avoid capsizing, but the boat was filling with water as Linnette frantically tried to row away from the castle.

Edris desperately began to bail out, but she had only her hands, she looked at the other boats moored on the jetty, but there was no way they could get back and fetch another.

Hurriedly she began to strip her armour.

"What are you doing?!" Linnette asked.

"We're going to swim," she said.

Linnette opened her mouth to protest but closed it again and nodded without a word. Edris knew it was dangerous, she couldn't risk losing her sword, or the Orb and yet she was going to plunge into freezing, cold water in the pitch-black. For a moment, she shook her head, wondering if it could get any worse.

At that moment, they heard a scream.

A loud, rage-filled scream, they turned to see Queen Ellawes standing at the water's edge. For a moment Edris was relieved, the beasts were gone, and they had a head start, even with a boat the Queen would struggle to catch up with them and she might never find them in the pitch-black lake, they could make it.

But as the Witch-Queen screamed, she changed.

Her body grew and her arms and legs warped into tentacles, first four, then six, then eight, then it seemed more than Edris could count. The Queen was growing all the time, seething and writhing.

The water in the boat was already too much, there was no way they could row any further. Edris looked at Linnette, in the dim light from the castle she seemed more beautiful and braver than ever. Edris sheathed her sword and held out her hand, then together they leapt into the ice-cold lake.

They began to swim, all the time heading away from the castle, away from whatever beast it was that the Queen had become.

But the beast was no longer on the water's edge; the Queen plunged into the lake with a great splash that echoed off the walls of the vast cave, streaming towards them all tentacles outstretched. Edris needed to swim faster, but with one hand holding the Orb and the other arm still in pain from the great blows she had given the stone beasts, she was struggling to keep up with Linnette, who was just a few paces ahead.

But then she was gone.

With barely a sound Linnette was sucked under the water and Edris was alone.

"Linnette!" she cried, hoping that somehow, she would reappear. But there was nothing. Edris turned around in the water, searching desperately.

But all she saw, almost as big as the castle itself, was the great towering kraken, a beast of giant clawed tentacles and a vast size that almost blocked out the little light there was.

Linnette was gone, Edris was lost, and the beast towered above her.

Suddenly there was a low rumbling growl, and the beast looked at her with its emerald eyes.

"Give back the Orb," it said.

"Never!" Edris shouted at the kraken, determined that she would do all within her power to get it back to her people.

She dove under the water, desperate to find Linnette but the blackness had enveloped her. There was no hope of finding anything.

Briefly, she broke the surface to catch her breath but before she went back into the dark water, something caught her eye. Not too far ahead; a light, a soft, reddish yellow light. The light of dawn bursting into the cave. Showing there was still a world outside, still a way out, still hope.

Edris tried to swim toward it but the kraken lashed out with a roar and dug a clawed tentacle into her back.

Screaming in shock and pain, she was dragged under. Her lungs empty, she struggled, hoping that the moment of light hadn't been the last time she would see the sun.

Edris knew that if she let go now, if she gave up and

allowed this beast to drown her, then she wouldn't be able to help Linnette and with that thought, she pulled the sword from its sheath and struck out at the tentacle that held her.

Released, she burst out of the water, gasping for air.

"Linnette!" she called, hoping that the girl had surfaced somewhere, that she would hear.

Suddenly she heard a scream.

Edris turned to look.

On the edge of the cave, emerging from the water and into the sunlight, was one of the stone beasts, it had run along the bottom of the lake and now it held Linnette, grasped in its jaws and shaking her like a rag-doll.

Suddenly it threw her from its mouth, Edris called out in horror as she watched helplessly. Linnette crashed against the cave wall and tumbled to the ground, her scream silenced, she lay motionless on the soft white sand, bathed in the morning light.

"No!" Edris called, weakly.

She made to swim to the water's edge, but the kraken was far from defeated, another of its great tentacles twisted around her body and pulled her under again. Edris struggled against it, her strength running out. Breaking the surface for a moment to gasp in precious air, she flailed, desperately trying to inch closer to the safety of the sandy bank, as the kraken struggled to suck her back under.

Edris could see sunlight, she could see Linnette, could see freedom, but she just couldn't reach it. She struggled against the kraken's strength but it wrapped around her, ever tighter, pinning her sword arm to her body, crushing her.

Edris pulled and twisted her body, fighting to keep her head above water but as another great hooked claw rose, and she looked into the monstrous face of what used to be the Witch-Queen, suddenly she knew what to do.

With the last of her strength, Edris threw the Orb, releasing her precious treasure and letting all hope out of her hand. She watched as it soared through the air and another of the kraken's claws hurtled towards it to grasp it and end everything.

The Orb broke through a sunbeam, landing next to Linnette on the sand, gleaming brightly in the sun.

Then there was silence.

Just the soft lapping of water.

The great talon of the beast had frozen just a hair's breadth from Edris' chest; solid and unmoving. She squeezed out from the hard rock that twisted around her body, extracting herself from what had, just a moment before, been a tentacle of a living beast, but was now nothing more than dead, unthinking stone.

She looked around the cave, lit by a piercing beam of sunlight. The castle beyond the lake seemed to be no more than shadows in the dark. The stone beast that had chased them all along the lake-bed was frozen in place, and there, still motionless on the sand, was Linnette.

Hurriedly Edris sheathed her sword and swam the last few feet towards the shore, her body heavy and tired, she ran toward the girl that had saved her life, but it was too late. Linnette's body was still and broken.

"You are free from your torment," she whispered softly, her voice breaking with tears.

With a heavy heart, Edris reached out to touch Linnette's face and in the bright light of day she realised her hand was marked with vivid red streaks, like a lightning bolt, where she'd held the Orb. She pulled up the sleeve of her tunic, the jagged lines ran up her arm twisting around like tentacles, pulsing red and still painful.

'A last curse of the wretched Orb,' she thought, bitterly.

She looked at the Orb where it lay in the sand, innocent, unmarked and unremarkable. It seemed incredible that something so small and innocuous could hold such power.

She wanted to throw the accursed thing into the water where it would never kill or hurt anything again. She reached out to snatch it but hesitated, knowing the pain it would cause her to hold it again. She steadied herself, taking a breath before grabbing it.

But rather than the lighting shock of pain she was expecting, it was warm. The heat soared up her arm. Suddenly the pain in her shoulders was gone, the ache in her limbs subsided. The crushed bones in her chest were relieved, and she remembered what it felt like to breathe normally, to feel no pain. Her body glowed with such warmth and joy that she laughed.

She looked down at Linnette. A desperate hope filled her, and she leant down, placing a gentle kiss upon her lips.

As she did so, the restorative warmth seemed to bubble and surge, flowing through her, through her body to her lip and into Linnette.

Within moments the cold, still body of Linnette was warm again, moving, breathing, and alive.

Edris pulled away and Linnette looked up at her, confused but living.

"What happened?" she asked, looking around.

Edris laughed in relief. "It's over!"

With one final glance at the kingdom in a cave, Edris wondered sadly what may have become of the Queen if she hadn't been so corrupted by the Orb's power. She turned away from the great dark shadows of rock and, taking Linnette's hand, they walked together into the sunlight.

Her eyes blinking and sore, Edris looked around the world for what felt like the first time and smiled as she saw her horse, Arrow, blithely eating grass by the edge of the wood, blissfully unaware of the adventure that had taken place.

She whistled for him and he looked up before bounding over more like a joyful puppy than a great armoured horse of the King's guard.

"Where will you go now?" Linnette asked suddenly, as Arrow nuzzled at Edris.

"Home, to my Kingdom. Where the Orb will be safe and used for good," she laughed at the thought, relieved that she could go home, relieved that she could save her people. But suddenly she wondered, "what about you?" she asked, realising that even after everything, she may still lose Linnette.

"I don't know." Linnette replied, "I lost my home, long ago."

"I'm sure Arrow is strong enough to carry us both," Edris said, and as though to demonstrate, she placed the Orb in a saddlebag and swung herself onto her horse's back, reaching out a hand to Linnette.

"If you're certain...?" Linnette said, cautiously.

"I wouldn't want it any other way," Edris replied, and with a smile, Linnette took her hand and leapt up behind Edris and together they rode home.

THE END

BREAKAWAY

S he dragged it along the cobbles. Having wheels meant the damned case was supposed to be easier to manage but it insisted on veering off into passing strangers.

Sarah had been led to believe that St Ives was a quiet Cornish fishing village, an artistic retreat, a quaint idyll. Instead, it was hot, loud and thronging with people.

Debbie had, of course, let her down. Apparently, she couldn't get away from Tom and the kids. Sarah hadn't bothered to read the whole e-mail, she'd just got on the train and decided to make the most of the weekend alone. But so far she was struggling to have fun.

When she finally reached the B&B she was sweaty, irritated, tired and ready to collapse.

She'd imagined the landlady as a scatty, old cat lady, with long purple scarves who only rented out rooms for the company, as she'd inherited a fortune and now whiled away her days painting abstracts and quoting poetry.

But she couldn't have been more wrong.

The woman who opened the door was wearing a pair of figure-hugging black jeans and a white shirt, her black hair had a slight curl to it and hung loosely about her shoulders in a way that reminded Sarah of a painting she'd once seen. Her eyes were a beautiful, bright green and her bare feet were the only hint that she was even slightly bohemian.

"Miss Deal?" Sarah asked, trying to stifle her surprise.

"Call me Jen" she smiled brightly holding out her hand "are you here about the room? Only I thought there were two of you."

Sarah's throat dried up, she wanted to say 'my secret lover can't get away from her husband this weekend so it's just little old me I'm afraid,' but instead she mumbled something about problems at work.

"Well not to worry, would you like to come and see your room? Oh and mind the cactus. I have no idea why I left it there."

A DAY AT AN ART GALLERY WAS JUST THE PEACE AND quiet she'd needed. It would give her a chance to think, contemplate and look at pretty things.

She was still angry at Debbie and hadn't responded to the late-night text offering excessive apologies and a promise to 'make up for it'. She was being made a fool of. She was so angry at herself for putting up with it and so angry with Debbie for making her feel guilty.

She was lost in thought when she caught sight of 'Jen' Deal staring at a colourful portrait of a Rhino balancing on a lemon. She hoped to squeeze past unnoticed; the last thing she needed was Jen's sunny disposition and those distractingly entrancing green eyes.

"Sarah!" 'Bugger'

"Jen! I didn't see you there!" The lie slithered off her tongue like a well-oiled snake.

" I didn't expect to see you inside on a gorgeous day like today, why aren't you out frolicking on the beach?"

'Frolicking?'

"Well I'm not really one for the crowds or the heat, or the beach come to think of it."

Jen laughed and leaned forward, conspiratorially.

"Well, I think you might have come to the wrong place!"

Sarah forced a smile and tried to think of a polite way of telling her to sod off.

"Come on I'll take you down to the beach and get you an ice cream. You look like you could do with cheering up."

She didn't want to be cheered up. She wanted to look at art and tell herself she was taking her mind off things whilst wallowing in self-pity and hate. But as she looked at those eyes, that smile and the soft black hair tucked delicately behind her ear, she felt herself melting and mumbled 'ok'.

Jen chattered away as she led Sarah down to the long white beach stretching along the horizon, the bright blue sky reflected in the clear water and the sound of waves was lost beneath a cacophony of shouting, screaming, and laughter.

Suddenly she was handed an ice-cream with a chocolate flake. She hadn't even noticed Jen getting it.

"Oh, you didn't have to!" She said as the ice cream started dripping onto her hand.

"My pleasure!" She took hold of Sarah's arm and led her down to the sea. "Now tell me Miss Sparks, and I do have to say that is a marvellous name, why have you travelled all the way down to lovely, sunny, practically-tropical

Cornwall only to wander around an art gallery looking like you've just been slapped?"

'Because I have just been slapped!' She thought, every time Debbie set her up then let her fall it was like a hard back slap across the face.

"I've always hated my name." She said, sidestepping the question.

"Really?! Why?! I think it's a brilliant name! Miles better than 'Deal', which might as well be 'Dull'."

"I nearly changed it once."

Jen looked at her with abject horror.

"NO! You can't! I love your name. I'd marry you just to get your name." Her tone suddenly changed. "Of course, there would be other reasons to marry you as well, I mean, I'm sure there would be other reasons to marry you, I mean... I should shut up now." It was the first time she'd seen Jen flustered and it felt great to realise that this gorgeous girl must have a crush on her.

But because she didn't think she deserved to feel great and because it was far too complicated to be liked by this girl, she decided to crush this crush. Immediately.

"I'm just upset that my girlfriend isn't here, you know. I really miss her." She looked at Jen, testing her reaction.

"Of course you do," Jen said; calmly and without any trace of disappointment or the good humour she'd had a few seconds before.

'Not so flippin' cheery now are we!?' Sarah thought, with twisted satisfaction and then immediate guilt and regret as she realised she actually liked her cheeriness.

"Do you want to go surfing?" Jen asked suddenly.

"Surfing?" She couldn't conceal her disdain.

"Yeah, only I've got a class later and it would be great if you could come."

Sarah desperately wanted to make up for that fleeting desire to crush her. Besides if Jen was taking a class she couldn't be that good, so it's not as if she could make a fool of herself.

———————

SHE WAS WRONG.

"I thought you meant" she hissed as Jen walked over "that you were taking a class, not that you were taking a class!"

"Does it matter? Now get down on that board" she said with unexpected authority "and let me see you jump."

The next few hours passed awkwardly. It was fine watching demonstrations; Jen's athletic body moved with elegance and even when she came off she did so with the grace of a Russian gymnast. Sarah, however, felt like a slightly unbalanced turtle in the midst of a group of synchronised dolphins. She felt like she was the only one struggling to get the knack of it and all she managed to achieve when she got in the water was a face full of sea. After the fortieth wipe-out she was exhausted and utterly powerless to get back on the board. Suddenly Jen was behind her. Sarah gasped as she felt gentle hands on her waist, they were comforting and warm but unexpected and she was surprised by her desire to be held tighter.

"Just hold it steady, jump, then slide on. Ready?" In a blind panic, Sarah leapt on the board, which promptly flipped her backwards and straight into the sea.

She went under, just for a moment but long enough for water to get sucked up her nose, her arms flailed but she managed to stand up quickly, still in panic-mode. Jen was next to her and although she'd been under as well, she laughed, a warm, heartfelt laugh.

"I'm no good at this," Sarah said, with more acceptance than defeat, and by the look on Jen's face, it was clear she agreed.

"Well, technically the class ended about ten minutes ago so no-one would think any worse of us if we called it a day."

The offer was too tempting to refuse and they walked back up to the house in their surf gear. Sarah was able to have a shower, get into some warm clothes and come downstairs in time to be served a gorgeous looking casserole.

"I know it's not traditional seaside fare, but I thought that, after today, you could do with something a bit more wholesome."

"Oh, I'm not complaining!" She said as she took the seat next to Jen and they chatted about their afternoon.

She liked hearing Jen laugh, she liked watching her as she talked and when she giggled she sat back in her chair and occasionally moved her hand up to cover her mouth, a move that Sarah found both sweet and elegant.

It seemed natural for the evening to continue with a bottle of wine and relocation to the sofa. Sarah's itinerary of local pubs and live music was quickly dropped in favour of staying in and watching Jen laugh, talk and then laugh some more.

The normally reserved Sarah put on a more tactile persona, placing her hand on Jen's arm at the punch-line of a joke or an intimate detail in a story. She wanted to be nearer to Jen, closer to this beautiful girl. But as they finished off the bottle, Sarah felt her moment was slipping away.

"Are you ok?" Jen must have noticed the look of concern.

She smiled and nodded, not taking her eyes from Jen's, she wanted to say something but there were no convenient words. Instead, she reached up and pushed back a loose lock of hair, her heart was throbbing in her chest as she stroked the soft skin of Jen's cheek.

Jen didn't back off and she didn't flinch; she looked at Sarah with unbroken gaze and then moved forward. They stared at one another, just a fraction apart, before finally they gave in and their lips brushed softly against one another.

Then the doorbell went.

———

SARAH RECOGNISED THE VOICE OF THE WOMAN TALKING to Jen at the door but she was still shocked when she emerged into the room. Her hair was perfect and her bright red lips matched her bright red nails, which matched her bright red luggage and her bright red scarf, which was draped dramatically around her shoulders.

"Debbie?! You came?" She managed to stutter.

"Of course I came darling, but if you don't mind I'd like to go to our room. I'm utterly exhausted."

Sarah put down her wine glass and led Debbie down the hall, carefully closing the door behind her.

"You should have told me you were coming!" She hissed. "I mean I'm delighted to see you, of course, I am, it's just... I can't keep being messed about like this. It's not good for us and it's not good for Tom and the kids. I mean, what have you told them?"

"I've left him."

"What!?"

"I ended it, I threw him out, told him everything. He went this afternoon and I came straight down to see you."

"But... That... God that's amazing!" She moved forward to take hold of the woman she'd wanted for her own, for so long, but she has brushed away.

"No one can know. Not yet... I still need time to get everything... sorted out."

"Get what sorted out? I mean it's over, isn't it? Finished? What is there to sort out?"

"Tom still owns a majority of the business and the house and with us working together... well, there are clearly going to be problems."

"In this day and age, it's not like anyone can say anything is it?"

"For God's sake Sarah!" her mood could change so quickly. "Isn't this what you wanted? Isn't this what you've been begging for, for months?"

"Yes... yes, of course, I just—"

"Well then stop bloody complaining!"

"I wasn't complaining I just—"

"Can't you just shut up and be happy? Do you have any idea what I've just given up for you?" She pulled out a cigarette.

"This is a no-smoking house..." she said without thinking "But I'm sure Jen won't mind." She added as Debbie lit up anyway.

"I'm ravenous," she said, clearly agitated "ask that woman to cook me something will you?"

"Jen's cooked already. I'll take you out somewhere."

Debbie sighed. "Fine, but I'll have to change."

Sarah just nodded and left the room. She needed a

chance to speak to Jen, to somehow explain. She caught her putting away the last of the crockery from dinner.

"I didn't know she was coming." She said, barely above a whisper.

"I know." Jen smiled brightly but continued cleaning.

"I actually thought we might be over, it's just that..."

"That you still love her. I understand of course I do."

"It's a little bit more complicated than that."

Jen stopped and looked up at her, the cheeriness had vanished.

"Sarah... I..."

"Are you coming like that?" Debbie appeared in the doorway looking fabulously glamorous in a red dress. Sarah glanced back at Jen still determinedly cleaning. The two women were so utterly different, the one she'd waited for and the one she wanted.

But she couldn't give up everything she held dear on a whim, a holiday fancy. She looked at Debbie, tall, gorgeous and so commanding, she had wanted this woman for so long and now she had her, she wasn't going to throw this away lightly. She made her decision and strode out of the house with Debbie, leaving Jen to her cleaning.

SHE DIDN'T SEE JEN WHEN THEY GOT BACK AND IN THE morning the breakfast was beautifully laid out, but Jen was already gone. Debbie complained incessantly about the appalling lack of service and it was all Sarah could do to keep silent.

They spent the day on the beach, Debbie constantly clicking her blackberry, Sarah staring over at the surfers. She was trying to pick out Jen amongst the horde. She thought she caught sight of her a few times, the familiar outfit and graceful movements, but then she was gone again, lost amidst the crowd.

It was a relief to get back to their room and start packing for home. She wanted to forget everything that had happened and stay focused on being happy with Debbie. She stayed in her room. She needed to avoid Jen and she made sure that they aimed for the earliest train so they could be out of the house before Jen was awake. Luckily Debbie was determined to get back into the city for a client meeting, so it didn't take much to usher her out of the door making them a good twenty minutes early for their train.

They dragged their luggage onto the long platform, and Sarah settled on a bench overlooking the beautiful, peaceful beach. It was hot and overhead the palm trees tousled in a whispering breeze; before her, the shore lapped serenely against the soft, white sand. She was going to miss the town, its pretty side streets, its quaint little shops and cafés, its stunning beaches and Jen. She was really going to miss Jen.

She gazed at Debbie, marching up and down the platform trying to compel her blackberry into receiving a signal. She thought of London, of the wide windows and bland grey views, of the strangling heat of the tube, of the manic rush of constantly angry people and she thought of Debbie; curt, authoritative, assertive Debbie. She would be with her all day, all evening, all night; Debbie and her blackberry.

She heard the distant train pulling up and suddenly she panicked. She stood, wanting to do something but not sure what.

Debbie strode over to her.

"The quicker we're out of this Godforsaken hole the better." She said, leaning down to grab her bag.

"I can't get on the train." Once the words were out, she knew they were true.

Debbie turned to her, confused.

"What do you mean? This is our train."

"I'm not coming back with you." She didn't care if she was doing the right thing. She just knew she couldn't do anything else.

"What do you mean Sarah? We've got to go back. We can't just take an extended holiday! This is so typical of you!" She was shouting over the noise of the train as it eased into the station.

"I can't go back; I can't go back with you. I'm sorry."

"You can't do this Sarah! Do you have any idea what I've lost because of you? Do you? I don't even have a home to go to because of you."

"What do you mean? I thought you threw Tom out" Debbie looked away and the realisation hit "he threw you out didn't he?" Sarah almost laughed, so many lies and yet she could still be fooled. "Did he do it because of us, or because he found out about one of your little schemes?"

"Look, we'll talk about this on the train." She grabbed hold of Sarah's wrist, but she pulled her arm free.

"I'm not coming with you, Debbie." And with that she felt it was over, she knew it was over, she knew she had broken their relationship for good and she was free.

Debbie stared at her for a moment before turning and stepping on the train. She was already back on her black-berry by the time the doors closed and the train heaved itself out of the station, leaving her alone on the platform staring at the beautiful, sun-drenched beach.

THE END

ENTHRALLED

S lowly, she counted to ten.

It was the only way to keep calm, focus her mind, and stop herself panicking. She couldn't afford to lose focus. She couldn't let ten months of arduous work slide from her hands.

The counting forced her to breathe and slowed her heart rate. Stella opened her eyes, rolled her neck to loosen it, then inched along the edge of the wall and peered around the corner.

There were a few scattered lamps but not enough to bathe the gardens in light, leaving pockets of darkness. This would be dangerous.

She switched to night vision, and the blackness became a fuzzy green landscape. She could just about pick out the trees and the low-lying walls.

There was no one about.

She could never be a hundred percent sure as there was only so much she could see with this gear. She'd wanted to invest in heat-sensitive equipment but wasn't even sure it would work on them. They didn't seem like the kind of creatures that were warm.

Stella checked her pistol and her crossbow. The serum was in her pocket, the knife was strapped tightly to her left thigh and, just as a precaution, she took out some oil and rubbed it onto her neck.

'Now or never,' she thought.

The Huntress took three short breaths then crawled out of her hiding place.

She stayed low as she made her way toward the electric fence. She took out the small disarming kit from one of her many pockets and found the wire buried beneath some grass at the fence post. She attached the disarmer, hiding her face as she set the charge. There was just a tiny explosion, but it was more than loud enough for one of them to hear. She had to go over immediately.

Tentatively she reached out and touched the fence. Nothing. It was fine. The electricity had gone. She shook it slightly. It seemed solid enough to climb over. She shimmied up and then swung herself over the top, landing with a thump on the other side.

She dashed into the undergrowth and waited, her crossbow at the ready.

Nothing came. Nothing even moved.

She knew she had to press ahead and began a slow crawl through the undergrowth, keeping low.

Stella had never heard of such a well-defended hive before and she had certainly never come close to one this big. She wondered how many there might be inside. In all her months of surveillance she had only ever seen one of them: the Queen. The one called 'Hedra'. But that didn't mean there weren't hundreds of them, like rats, crawling all over the building.

She shuddered at the thought. She had no idea what she was going to be greeted by when she got inside. If she got inside.

If this had been anyone else, she would have told them they were mad to go in alone. All hunters should have backup; even with their extra strength none of them could tackle a hive even half this size alone.

But Stella had no choice.

She came to the edge of the undergrowth. There was a lawn between her and the house. She knew it was clear of landmines as she'd seen a gardener mowing it during her surveillance, but it would still be dangerous to cross. If there were patrols out, then she was as good as dead. Even on this moonless night, in this pitch blackness, to one of them it was as good as broad daylight; she would be seen in an instant.

Stella looked around, trying to think of another way. She could try edging further along the undergrowth: some if it came close to the house. But she was still going to have to cross the lawn at some point. The only other way up to the house would be the driveway, but she might as well ring the doorbell for all the cover it would give.

It would have to be the lawn and it would have to be now.

She readied her crossbow, just in case. Keeping a close eye out for anything that moved, she stepped tentatively onto the lawn. The Huntress stood perfectly still for a moment, waiting to see if she was going to be swooped upon. Then she made a run for it. She sprinted at full pelt across the grass and leapt onto the gravel path surrounding the house.

At the sound of gravel underfoot she leapt into the flower beds, hoping that no one had heard that one step, that one stupid mistake, and that no one would come looking.

She would have to keep moving, if they came to investigate there was nowhere to hide: she was completely exposed.

'Left or right?' she thought.

One way led to the front of the house, the other to the back. They could come from either direction, but the safer option would be to head to the back. She hoped she was right and took off at a steady run, diving around the corner of the building.

She stopped, crouching low and listening to the darkness. It was difficult to make out her surroundings through the green haze of her night vision goggles. There were shapes and shadows everywhere but she couldn't work any of them out. She crept along, keeping close to the wall. There was a light up ahead, streaming out of one of the windows. Silently she made her way towards it and sat underneath.

She removed her goggles and rubbed her face: they were no good for light and she needed to look through that window. She knew she was taking a risk by looking in, she knew she could be seen. But this whole expedition was a risk, and it wouldn't be worth the risk if she didn't make damned sure it worked.

She breathed slowly, pacing herself and calming her mind. A huntress needed to be able to think if something happened, she couldn't rely on adrenaline; it would cloud her judgement. If there was about to be a battle, she had to make sure she was prepared for it. She double-checked the bolt on her crossbow, pulling it back and locking it. It was her favourite weapon. It was cumbersome and awkward, it had to be reloaded with every shot, but it worked. If you hit them right, it damn well worked.

Slowly she turned, kneeling under the window. She rose and peered over the window ledge, keeping low, keeping out of sight, hoping that it would be enough to avoid being seen by those sharp and malevolent eyes of theirs.

She let out a gasp as she realised she was just a few feet away from her.

The Queen.

There was just enough light for her to see. They were both there: the Queen and her thrall. It made her stomach squirm. It had been so long, so long since she had seen her, so long since she had been this close. Even in all those months of tracking, she had never got this close to her.

It had been an obsession. It was all that kept her going; it had consumed her until there was nothing left but the hunt. And now she was here, just an arm's reach away from her, and she wanted to get closer, she had to get closer.

To Stella, the Queen was nothing but a leech. Sucking the lifeblood from her victim, keeping them in a thrall the way a spider keeps a fly in its web, keeping them alive only for the convenience of fresh blood. It made her sick.

She watched them, the Queen and her victim. It hurt to watch her, to see such a beautiful young woman reduced to a doe-eyed fool worshipping at the feet of a parasite. But Stella knew she was under a thrall, knew it was just a hypnotic trance, a love potion capable of warping even the strongest of minds into believing it must obey its mistress.

The Queen leaned in, stroking her victim's cheek. She was going to drink. Stella was repulsed; she couldn't let it happen. She couldn't stand by and watch even one more drop of blood be taken.

She smashed the window.

They looked up in shock as the Huntress fired the crossbow. It hit the Queen, square in the chest, and she fell to the floor.

"Felicity!" Stella called, as she climbed over the sill.

"Stella?" The woman looked from the Queen to the Huntress, confused and terrified.

She didn't have time to explain: she grabbed hold of Felicity and started to drag her away.

"Stella! What are you doing!?"

"I need you to come with me. Now!"

Stella looked at the Queen, she was already starting to recover; she'd missed the heart. But she didn't have time to load another bolt. She pulled Felicity to the window, they could still escape.

"I'm not going anywhere!" Felicity shouted as she tried to get back to her Queen.

But Stella knew it was just the thrall. She knew it was how they all acted, she had been prepared for this. But she shouldn't have made her move so soon: she should have stayed down, waited for a better moment. She shouldn't have been irrational, should have just watched her take the blood.

The Queen was half-standing. Felicity wrenched her arm from Stella's grasp and went to help her up. Stella loaded another bolt but before she could fire it, the Vampire was there. She pulled the crossbow out of the Huntress's hands and threw it across the room.

"Get out of my house!" the Queen screamed.

"Not empty-handed."

Quickly, Stella drew her knife.

The Queen leapt backwards as Stella swiped the knife across her stomach. It barely touched her. But she followed it up with a sharp left hook to the Queen's jaw and, in her weakened state, the Vampire was knocked to the ground.

Stella ran, grabbing Felicity by the arm, pulling her from the room and into the hall, heading toward the front door. But the Queen was fast on their heels.

Suddenly, Felicity pulled free and dashed up the stairs. The Huntress turned to see the Vampire mid-leap, teeth bared. She swung the knife blindly, just as the Queen landed on her. She wrestled the wounded Queen to the floor before dashing up the stairs after Felicity.

She was running down the corridor and Stella followed her at full pelt. She ran into a room and tried to slam the door, but Stella threw herself against it, jamming her foot against the frame. She forced it open, pushing her way into the room, then bolted the door and leaned against it, breathing heavily.

"What are you doing here?!" Felicity shouted. "Get out!" She was angry and panicked.

"Felicity... Listen to me," Stella said, trying to sound calm despite gasping for air. She stepped forward, trying to show she wasn't a threat. But she had to remind her, had to explain.

"It's me. It's Stella. I've come to rescue you."

"I know who you are, Stella. I don't need rescuing, I told you before: it's over between us!"

"You're in a thrall," she said as if talking to a child. She knew it would be a lot for her to take in, knew it would be hard for her to understand. "The Queen, Hedra," she continued, "you've been hypnotised by her. It's okay; I know this must be confusing for you."

Felicity was backing away, heading toward the window. Suddenly there was banging on the door.

"GET OUT OF THERE!" It was the Queen, demanding back her prey.

"Hedra!" Felicity shouted.

"Shh it's okay, she won't get you," said Stella, stepping forward, following Felicity to the window. "I won't let her get you."

"You're mad!"

"I've tracked you for months, Felicity. I've followed you both everywhere, waiting for my move, waiting for the chance to get you back. There hasn't been a day when I haven't thought of you."

"Well, get over it!"

Felicity pulled at the lock on the window, desperately trying to open it. The banging at the door continued; the Queen was starting to break it down. Stella was running out of time.

"I know it's hard to believe, but your mind isn't clear."

"My mind is perfectly clear, Stella. Hedra is going to break through that door any moment and if she thinks you've hurt me, she'll–"

"It's okay, it's okay. Look." She pulled the serum from her pocket and held it up. "I have this."

"What is it?" Felicity asked, looking worried, but curious.

"It's a serum. It was hell to get hold of it, but it reverses the effect of the thrall."

"I'm not under a thrall, Stella! Deal with it: I fell in love with someone else!"

"I know that's how it feels, I know that's what you think right now, but just take the serum and all this will be over."

The door burst open, and the Queen flew through, knocking Stella to the ground. The serum fell from her hand; she scrabbled around for it as the Queen landed another blow to the back of the head and dragged her to her feet, holding her up with one hand.

"Hedra, be careful with her," Felicity said.

Stella was dazed and trying to blink back her vision as the knife was torn from her hand and thrown across the room.

"Maybe I should put you under a thrall," the Vampire spat.

"I would never serve you," Stella said, her strength starting to return.

"I wouldn't give you a choice."

The Queen spun her around, sinking her teeth into her neck. Stella felt a sharp pain and then numbness, before she was thrown to the floor. She looked up, smiling; the Queen was spitting the blood from her mouth.

"Anointing oil," said Stella standing, as the Queen started to cough.

"Hedra!" Felicity rushed to her aid as she collapsed.

Stella seized the serum and then grabbed Felicity, pulling her from the room.

"What did you do to her!?" Felicity screamed.

"I poisoned my neck! Come on!" Stella pulled her out of the front door and onto the lawn. "Quickly!" she said, pulling the stopper off the serum. "Drink this."

"I'm not under any thrall!"

"Then prove me wrong!" She looked at her in desperation. Looked at the Felicity she had known and loved; that Felicity was in there somewhere, she knew it, buried deep under this hypnotised shell. She was there, screaming to get out, and this was her only chance.

"Please, Felicity," she whispered, "just drink it." Felicity took the bottle from Stella's hand and looked at her for a moment. "Please."

They knew the Queen was on her way, she would be here any second. But the instant she drank the serum it would be over. Stella would have her Felicity back, they could leave the parasite to find another victim. Felicity took a breath and then gulped it back.

Instantly, she doubled over. It was taking effect, Stella hadn't warned her about the taste, or the reaction, but it didn't matter, she had taken it. She dropped to her knees, in too much pain to even cry out.

"Just a few seconds more," Stella said, gently touching her shoulder.

"Get away from her!"

The Vampire was running toward them across the grass. Stella went for her pistol but it was too late: the Vampire threw her to the ground and landed a punch to her jaw. Stella kicked her off and unhooked her pistol, but almost instantly she was pounced on again.

As the claws of the Vampire Queen dug into her flesh, Stella saw Felicity in the throes of the serum. She knew that any moment now she would be free.

Stella scrabbled around, reaching her hands out desperately for something, anything, as the Vampire's grip tightened around her neck. She grabbed a handful of dirt and gravel, throwing it into the Queen's face. The grip loosened and Stella threw her off.

She scrambled up, finally pulling the pistol from her holster.

"Silver bullets," she said with a smile, looking down at the Vampire crouched on the lawn.

"Stella, no!"

Felicity leapt in front of Hedra but it was too late, she'd pulled the trigger.

It took them a moment to react. Felicity looked down at

her chest: her breathing was rapid and ragged. She put her hand up to cover the wound, to try to stem the flow of blood.

Stella lowered the gun. She didn't understand, she couldn't understand how or why Felicity had jumped in front of the Vampire.

Felicity fell backwards into Hedra's arms.

"Flik?" said Hedra, softly looking down at her.

Felicity tried to answer, tried to speak, but no words came out.

"No, no, no, Flik! Please..." Hedra said, rocking her gently. "You can't! Please!" She lay her on the ground, holding the wound. There was so much blood flowing, she was trying to apply pressure, but she was panicking.

"Why did you do it, Flik? Why? It wouldn't have killed me; the bullet wouldn't have killed me..." She was trying to hold back, but she started to sob.

Felicity reached up, stroking Hedra's cheek.

"I... love you..." she managed. Before her arm fell back to the ground. She was gone.

The Queen let out a howl, clutching the body of her lover to her chest as Stella looked on, still holding the pistol. Still struggling to understand. The serum should have worked, it should have removed the thrall, it should have removed all traces of the thrall.

If she had been under a thrall.

Stella dropped to her knees, finally realising what she had done.

"I didn't know," she whispered.

"She told you," said the Queen, "she told you to leave her alone, you didn't listen."

"Kill me," Stella whispered.

Hedra looked at her and shook her head slowly. She

stood, heaving the body of Felicity off the ground and standing over Stella.

"Unlike you," she said, "I am not a murderer." Then she turned and carried the body back to the house.

THE END

IS SHE?

"My feet hurt."

"You shouldn't have worn heels," Mandy snapped.

"I didn't know we'd be walking so far!" Claire whined.

"Well, you insisted we go shopping! I wanted to go straight there, but no, you said 'let's go down Oxford Street,' 'let's look at shoes and dresses and hats,'—"

"You enjoyed it!"

"I come all this way so you can look at a load of random houses, and this is the thanks I get!"

"You came for shopping!"

They continued to bicker all the way down Denmark Street and it was only when they reached the other end that they realised they'd missed the turn.

"You've got the map!" Mandy said.

"Yes, but everything in real life looks so different to how it is on paper!"

Mandy shook her head and turned around, pulling the map from Claire and heading back down the road, looking for the turn to Carlton Road. Claire followed, hauling her bags along with her.

Claire wasn't angry, she could never be really angry with her. They were best friends; she wasn't sure what she would do without her.

Of course, things hadn't always been quite so easy between them.

It was Mandy that had made Claire realise, and learn to come to terms with the fact, that she was gay. She'd been in love with Mandy since she was thirteen, but had long come to accept that her feelings were unrequited. When she was seventeen, she had eventually gained the courage to come out and Mandy had accepted it, without hesitation and their friendship had grown stronger.

Now that Claire was moving to London to go to university, she knew it would change everything, and she had been so relieved when Mandy agreed to come with her to view houses. She'd been terrified of going on her own and just knowing that she'd have Mandy with her had made things so much easier. Twenty-Three Carlton Road was the last place on her list. It was the cheapest, but it was, by far, the furthest away from college and she already had a mind to turn it down.

Mandy rang the bell and when the door opened, Claire looked up to see a tall, dark, beautiful girl standing behind it. She had long, straight, black hair which looked smooth and silky as it flowed over her shoulders. Her eyes were dark, almost black, her skin was soft, the colour of caramel, and she wore a gold necklace and earrings, but rather than be garish, the jewellery made her look like an Egyptian Princess.

"We're here to see the room," Mandy said, as it became clear that Claire wasn't going to say a word.

"Oh right, ok well, do come in."

"We've been shopping," Mandy said, seeing the girl's questioning look as they struggled over the threshold with bags upon bags filled to bursting with stuff.

"Yes, I can see," she smiled and Claire felt butterflies spinning in her stomach. "I'm Jasmine, and you must be Claire," she said, holding out her hand to Mandy.

"No, I'm Mandy, I just came for the shopping. This is Claire."

Claire managed a small awkward wave but, for some reason, she had completely forgotten how to speak.

"Nice to meet you, shall I take you straight up?"

They both nodded and Jasmine turned and led them down the hallway. The carpet was old and threadbare, Claire wasn't sure she could tell what colour it was supposed to be, there were so many patches and stains she wasn't sure there was any of the original colour left. The wallpaper wasn't much better, there were gaps where it had been ripped off and there was an ominous-looking damp patch near the ceiling. But she said nothing and followed Jasmine up the flight of stairs onto a landing.

Rather than stopping, they continued up another flight of stairs onto the next landing. Claire was relieved when Jasmine went to open a door, but behind it was just another set of stairs. Claire summoned all the energy she could muster and followed her up the small winding set of steps.

"It's quite a long way up," Mandy said.

"Yes, it is," replied Jasmine, "I don't often come up here, my room is on the first floor, but there is a beautiful view up here."

As she spoke, she opened the door to a low-ceilinged room. It was cramped but there was a double bed and a large chest of draws, Mandy went straight over to the cupboard. But Claire followed Jasmine to the window.

She was right, it was a beautiful view. Claire could see all the different parts of London; in the distance, she could see the Gherkin and on the other side of the city, she could see the London eye. But all the rooftops between her and the river made her think of the scene in Mary Poppins when all the chimney sweeps come out to dance.

"It's beautiful," Claire whispered, turning to catch Jasmine looking straight at her and smiling softly. Her eyes bright, and yet dark, her smile subtle, yet radiating light from within her.

"Yes, it is," she whispered back.

"You can't even put a hanger in this cupboard," Mandy said, breaking the moment.

"The chest of drawers is really quite big," Jasmine said, "and if there is anything that needs to be hung up there is a cupboard on the landing that's never used." She swept out of the room. "I'll show you the rest of the house," she called.

"I don't like this place," Mandy whispered.

"Yes, she's lovely."

They followed Jasmine back down the three flights of stairs, struggling along with their bags. But despite the difficulty, Claire couldn't help but admire the way Jasmine's body moved, the way her hips swayed in her long, loose shirt.

Jasmine stopped to open a small door. "This is the bathroom."

Claire had at least been expecting to see a bath in the bathroom, instead, it was just a tiny little cupboard with a toilet, a sink, and a shower. It was cold and damp and it didn't look like there was even enough room to get changed in there.

"Is there just one bathroom for everyone?" Mandy asked, aware that there were six bedrooms in the house.

"Yes, but everyone has different schedules, so you rarely get a queue." Jasmine smiled and Claire couldn't help but relax.

"Well that seems fine then," Claire said, dreamily.

"If we go down here, I'll take you to the kitchen," Jasmine continued.

She led them down a dark stairway that led to the cellar; it looked like the type of place the protagonist in a horror film should never go into.

Jasmine opened a door and light spilt into the dingy little stairwell. Despite being in the cellar, the kitchen had french windows opening onto a small set of concrete steps leading up to an overgrown garden. The windows rattled slightly in the wind and Claire wondered how easy it would be for passing animals or criminals to get through them. She brushed off the thought and tried to think of the positive. Which was difficult in a kitchen that looked as though it had been through the blitz.

All the furniture was ancient, the cupboards that were stuck to the walls wouldn't have looked out of place in a museum. The sink was grimy and piled high with washing up, a rickety old ironing board had been left out and the oven looked as though it could burst into flames at any moment out of sheer misery.

"Well, I think you've given us plenty to think about," Mandy said, "Thank you so much for showing us around, but we really have to be getting on."

"It's not a problem," Jasmine said, "I'll show you out." She took them back up the cramped stairs and towards the heavy front door. "You have my email," Jasmine continued, "so if you have any questions, just give me a shout." She opened the door for them and they scrambled through with their bags. "Take care."

"Bye," said Claire as she headed down the steps and back onto the street.

"Thanks," Mandy called.

Claire turned to wave and just caught sight of Jasmine smiling at her as she closed the door. The moment she was gone Claire felt a tugging, deep in the pit of her stomach.

They left Carlton Road and made their way back to Denmark Street. They looked up the long road, there was no way they were going to be able to walk all the way back. They would collapse in a heap of shopping bags and shoes before they got halfway.

"BUS!" shouted Mandy.

Claire looked and sure enough, rattling towards them was an old red London bus. They took a run for it, flailing their arms wildly trying to catch the driver's attention. The bus careened towards a shelter and stopped to let off a few passengers. Claire and Mandy ran up just in time to scramble on and wave their day pass at the unresponsive driver before he took off once again.

They hauled their bags up onto the top deck where they could flop down, taking up two seats each. Claire fell back, delighted to have the weight off her feet and immediately started thinking about when she might next be able to see Jasmine.

"Well that house is definitely off the list," Mandy started, "the flat in Camden is my favourite and I know you liked that one too, plus the rent is still cheap—"

"I'm taking it," Claire announced, utterly certain that she was doing the right thing.

"Good, I was worried there for a moment that you might be mad enough to—"

"If Jasmine lives there, it can't be that bad."

"You're taking Carlton Road! You can't be serious—"

"Mandy?"

"What?"

"We're on the wrong bus!"

AFTER SHE WAVED HER DAD OFF, CLAIRE TURNED TO look at all the boxes lining the tiny corridor. She hadn't wanted to let either of her parents see the state of the house she had chosen, but now she was left with the task of heaving all of her worldly possessions up a million flights of stairs alone. She bent down and lifted the first box, wondering why on earth she had decided to bring so much with her. What could she possibly want with all the Harry Potter books (adult version, hardback) and four different hair dryers?

As she walked across the landing on the first floor, she looked longingly at Jasmine's bedroom, wondering when she would see her again. She didn't have to wait long.

"Hey!" Jasmine said brightly as she opened her door.

Claire tried to look casual while perched halfway up the stairs holding a box that was slipping through her fingers. "Hey," she said.

"Do you need a hand?"

"No, it's fine," she lied.

"Nonsense. I'll grab the next box and meet you up there." She smiled and Claire couldn't help but smile back before finishing the struggle up to the top room.

Even with Jasmine's help it still took them the best part of an hour, going up and down, with box, after box, after box of stuff, upon stuff. But to her credit, Jasmine didn't complain once.

As Claire dragged the last box into her room and dropped it on the floor, she thought she would just collapse. She slumped onto her new bed, exhausted. She could worry about emptying the boxes later, for now, she didn't want to move.

"How about a nice cup of tea?" Jasmine asked. She stood by the door ready to go downstairs, seemingly unaffected by all the heavy lifting and running up and down.

"That would be lovely," Claire said, 'if you could just bring it to me while I lay here and die,' she thought, but she dragged herself up and followed Jasmine.

However, they didn't go all the way down to the kitchen, instead, they stopped on the first floor and Jasmine invited her into her bedroom. Claire got a fluttering of butterflies as she crossed the threshold into the other girl's room. It was surprisingly lovely in Jasmine's room; there was no trace of the unpleasantness in the rest of the house as if Jasmine had created her own little oasis.

There were posters and pictures all over the walls, a heaving bookshelf, trinkets, make-up, and the mild smell of incense. Claire noticed a small sink in the corner and a chest of drawers kitted out like a kitchen with a microwave and a kettle that Jasmine flicked on.

"I try to avoid using the downstairs kitchen," she said, by way of an explanation.

That made sense, the kitchen wasn't exactly the nicest place Claire had ever seen, but Jasmine's reluctance to use it did make her wonder. "If you don't mind me asking," Claire said, hoping Jasmine wouldn't think she was being too intrusive "what made you take this place?"

"Money." She sighed, "I had..." Jasmine paused, trying

to find the right words, "I had a bit of a falling out with a... friend, last year. We'd taken a tiny one-bedroom flat in Bloomsbury and then she moved out, so I was stuck there. It was far too small for me to advertise for a roommate, so I had to pay all the rent myself for six months. It crippled my savings and meant I had to take the cheapest place I could find."

"Oh, I'm sorry to hear that." Claire wanted to know more about this 'friend' and she wanted to find out everything about Jasmine. But didn't want to seem too eager, or invasive, so she decided not to probe further "who else lives here?"

"There's a couple of artists, Jamie and Danni, an economist, Graham and a Dutch PhD student, Marissa... She's studying anthropology, I think. She's really interesting, but hardly ever around."

Claire wondered if that meant that the artists and the economist weren't interesting. But she didn't have a chance to ask, the kettle boiled and Jasmine turned to attend to the tea.

"Would you like milk?" Jasmine asked, "Only I have to fetch it from downstairs."

"I have a mini-fridge," Claire said, thinking of all the stuff she had brought with her.

"Sorry?"

"I have a mini-fridge," she repeated, but knew how bizarre the statement was, "for the milk," she added, "if you want it... only there's no sink in my room so... I mean I'd only use it for soft drinks and I don't really like soft drinks... so if you wanted it to complete your little kitchen you could use it... as a thank you... for the tea," Claire realised that giving someone a fridge (however small) in exchange for tea was a tad dramatic, "and for helping me with all my stuff...

and I wouldn't feel so bad about popping in and saying hello," she was rambling and she knew it, "you know... if I'm passing and want to avoid the kitchen," she had to make herself stop speaking, "I could come in... and say 'hi'," she had to stop, "... to the fridge..." nope, it was too late, she was now officially a 'nutter.'

"That would be nice," Jasmine said without a hint of sarcasm, "but for now I'll just pop downstairs and grab the milk."

'What the hell was I jabbering about?' Claire thought as Jasmine left. She felt like a wittering idiot, she couldn't think why she always felt the desperate need to just talk. Talk, talk, talk all the flipping time! She forced herself to look at the books on Jasmine's shelves, hoping there might be something there that she would recognise and they could talk about.

However, most of the books were a mystery to her, she hadn't heard of half the words in the titles; let alone the actual contents of the books. There was hardly anything on the shelves that seemed as though she would want to read it. Then one book caught her eye. It was a black book, there was nothing written on the spine. Curiously she pulled it out. In gold letters on the front was written the word 'Journal.' Trembling, knowing she shouldn't, knowing it was wrong, knowing that it went against everything right, she opened the book.

She only caught a couple of words written clearly on the newest entry before she heard footsteps on the stairs. Hurriedly she thrust the book back where she had found it, now desperate to know more of the contents.

"Milk!" Jasmine said as she entered.

Claire tried not to look at the diary again, tried not to make it obvious that she had looked inside and seen those words. She had to try to get herself to think of other things, but all she could focus on was the possibility... maybe... could she be?

"Sugar?" Jasmine asked with a smile.

"Yes!" Claire said, a little too enthusiastically. "Two, if that's ok?"

"That's fine." Jasmine handed her the mug and sat down next to her on the bed. She was just a few inches away. Claire was sitting with Jasmine, on her bed. This was better than she could have hoped for on the first day.

"So, it's philosophy that you study? Right?" Claire tried to keep her tone neutral and calm, she wanted to seem casual but she didn't want to let on that she had been internet stalking Jasmine from the moment she had met her, desperately trying to find out everything she could about her.

"Yeah, it's quite interesting, but there is SO much reading and so many clashing ideas. You have to keep a completely open mind."

'Open mind'? Was she trying to say she was 'open-minded', was she trying to communicate her willingness to be open-minded about certain things?

"I'm quite open-minded about things," Claire said, trying to hint, but not certain exactly what she was hinting at. This was rubbish. She was doing badly. Really badly.

"Well, that's good." Jasmine looked at her, with her dark eyes and her seductive smile just playing across her lips.

Claire felt her face get hot and looked away. 'Maybe this is going well,' she thought, 'maybe this is going really well'.

"I have to go and finish unpacking," Claire said, unable to think of anything else to say, and cursing herself for ending their meeting so quickly "thanks for the tea."

"Not a problem," Jasmine said, taking back the still full cup, "feel free to pop in anytime."

"I will!" She shut her mouth before she started wittering again and left with a quick wave. She ran upstairs to her bedroom, she had to talk to Mandy; she had to talk to her now.

She found her phone lying on the floor under her handbag and quickly dialled Mandy's number; she barely let Mandy greet her before she blurted it out. "I think Jasmine might be gay!"

"What makes you think that?"

"She made me tea—"

"Tea makes you gay now, does it?" Mandy replied scornfully.

"and when I looked in her diary—"

"You looked in her diary?"

"When I looked, I know I saw the phrase 'she's beautiful,' not 'he's beautiful,' not 'it's beautiful,' definitely 'she's beautiful,' so I think that's a good indicator."

"Look, for one thing, you should not be reading that, and for another thing... ," Mandy was going into 'rant-mode.' "She could be talking about anything: a baby, a puppy, a celebrity. Even if she is talking about a friend, or whatever, it doesn't mean that she is gay; girls can still recognise that other girls are attractive."

"So, what do you think I should do? How do you think I should find out? Do you think I should try to get hold of the diary and read the rest of it?

"No, Claire—"

"She'll be going out soon and she must have a lot of lectures so I could pick the lock."

"Claire!"

"I've seen it in films; they have to use a hat pin or a hair clip or something."

"Claire!?"

"But if she writes in a code, then I'd have to crack it, but she can't write in code unless the 'beautiful' thing was a code for something else—"

"CLAIRE!"

"What?"

"You are NOT breaking into her room and stealing her diary!" Mandy shouted "that's insane! Just be friends, get to know her, be patient!"

"I can be patient" Claire replied, full of enthusiasm for her new mission, "I can do that!"

"Good."

"Exactly how long do I have to be patient for?"

CLAIRE HAD A LIST, AS LONG AS HER ARM, OF ALL THE things she ought to be reading for class.

She told herself that she was just taking a five-minute break, but she had already spent the last two hours scouring the internet for information, advice, 'how to's,' anything that could help her.

She had seen the words 'she's beautiful' written clearly at the end of Jasmine's last diary entry. Although she didn't have an opportunity to read the rest, she felt sure that this was significant. This was a sign of something, she was meant to stumble on it, she was meant to find out.

'After all,' she thought 'don't people have loads of crazy stories about how they met? About how fate pulled them together? Perhaps this is what was happening here, perhaps fate led me to this house, to that journal entry... to that girl. To Jasmine...'

But she needed confirmation. She needed to know for sure!

She had typed 'how do you tell if a girl is a lesbian' into a search engine and had come up with pages and pages and pages and PAGES of results. It appeared everyone, everywhere had an opinion on it. They all seemed to have a tip or a trick that was sure to work, sure to give you an answer.

Claire decided that she would make a note of them all and then the signs which were most commonly mentioned were sure to be most important. Plus, if she started to see a lot of signs that related to Jasmine then she would know she was onto something.

'But how to confirm it?'

So far, top of her list was 'short hair' this was one of the most common signs but it didn't apply to Jasmine, so it was a bit frustrating. The next most common was; 'wearing boys/men's clothes.' She hadn't seen Jasmine in anything that could be men's but she would keep an eye out for it.

Another thing on the list was something that seemed obvious now that she had been told, and that was 'they talk about girls... a lot'. Claire hadn't had much of a chance to really talk to Jasmine, so she had put that on her 'to look out for' list.

Sport looked like it was essential. Lesbians like football, hockey, lacrosse, cricket, tennis, and roller-skating. A few websites were adamant that lesbians don't like horse riding, but there were just as many places that said they did, so Claire put that down on the signs list as a maybe.

There was a lot of stuff about rainbows; rainbow flags, rainbow posters, rainbow key rings, rainbow badges. Again, she hadn't seen Jasmine wear or display any rainbows, but she would pay close attention from now on.

Claire found a few people who all mentioned the same things about wearing silver rings. She knew that Jasmine had some gold jewellery and now she would keep an eye out for her wearing a silver ring. People were very specific about which finger the ring ought to be on, but they were all suggesting different fingers, so, for now, she would ignore that bit.

Then Claire hit the jackpot: a few places suggested lesbians tie their hair in ponytails which are secured at the nape of the neck. This was exactly how she had seen Jasmine tie her hair the days she helped her move in! This was a definite sign! It was the first one on the list that she could put a big green tick next to. She looked down the list of other things she would have to check and felt sure that they were all within reach. Soon she would be able to prove, without a shadow of a doubt, that Jasmine was definitely gay.

Her phone buzzed. It was a message from Mandy.

'Job interview done by 5pm. Can I come over for dinner after?'

'Definitely! I'll have it ready for six!'

The minute she sent it she regretted it. She realised it was going to be an absolute nightmare getting the kitchen up to a standard where she could have dinner in it. She would have to work fast.

Claire spent the next few hours avoiding reading and instead, cleaning the kitchen and bathroom. She tried moving some of the furniture around so that the table could at least have people sitting at it, rather than being pushed into a corner with a load of junk on top. Then she used her own saucepans and her own utensils rather than the unpleasant 'house' ones and was close to making a passable curry when the doorbell rang.

When she led Mandy into the kitchen her reaction was of pleasant surprise; saying it looked much better than she remembered it. Claire beamed internally. It still gave her a little buzz to get praise from Mandy and she started talking her through all the research she had conducted into the signs hoping she would praise her for her hard work and dedication.

"It's not exactly a science, is it?" Mandy said.

"How did the interview go?" Claire decided that changing the subject was the best way to deal with her disappointment. Her curry looked as though it was vaguely finished, so she ladled it out onto two matching plates.

"Well, it's a bit confusing, really."

"So," said Claire, laying their hot plates on the table "talk me through it."

Mandy sighed as she began relating her tale, the jobs she wanted were scattered across the country and the interviews were expensive to get to and difficult to prepare for, plus she had to keep taking time off from her current job to attend. Today's interview had gone really well, and they had practically offered her the job at the end which was fantastic, but she would still have to wait for confirmation.

"Hey," said Mandy, breaking off to greet Jasmine as she walked into the room. Claire's stomach immediately jolted at the prospect of being in the same room as her again.

"Heya," Jasmine replied.

"So, I think I'll still go to the interview for the one at Colby's," Mandy continued, "I mean the worst thing that could happen is that I'll get them both and will be able to choose, what do you think?" Mandy looked at Claire who was gazing across the room. "Claire? What do you think?"

But it was no use. Claire wasn't listening. She was looking at Jasmine, her cheeks were flushed and she had a nervous smile on her lips, then, when Jasmine turned to speak to her, she could barely articulate a reply.

"So, what are you two up to?"

"Food," said Claire, stupidly.

"I had an interview in the City," Mandy said, stepping in, "And Claire graciously offered to cook dinner for me. How about you? Any plans for this evening?"

"I'm actually meeting a friend down on the Southbank. I love it down there, we might go to the globe or something, have you ever been?" Jasmine leant against the sink and started to peel an orange. Claire couldn't take her eyes off Jasmine's hands, her skin looked so soft and the way she delicately moved her fingers made Claire wish she could be that orange.

"No," said Mandy, forced to step in again "neither of us have really been around London much, we could do with a tour of the best bits!"

"We'll have to do that one weekend; I could take you to all the secret places the tourists never find!" She winked conspiratorially.

"That would be great!"

"Well, have a lovely evening!" Jasmine said as she left.

"You too!" Mandy called after her.

"Did you see what she was wearing?" Claire hissed as if Jasmine was still in the room.

"What about it?"

"Doc Martens!" Claire announced "She was wearing Doc Martens! That was one of the signs, lesbians wear Doc Martens, so... Jasmine could be gay!"

"For God's sake, Claire!" Mandy snapped "You are

completely mad! Not one of these so-called signs applies to you!"

Claire stared at Mandy blankly for a moment. When she spoke it was as if to a child, "but I know I'm gay, I don't need to look for signs about me..."

Mandy threw her head back in frustration "Exactly!" she said "You are gay, but you have none, not one, of those stupid signs you're so obsessed with. Doesn't that tell you that maybe the signs are complete rubbish? It's not about how you dress, or how you walk or what sport you play or how dumb you are, you just fall in love with who you fall in love with!"

Claire looked at her "but... then how do I find out?"

"Oh, just open your bloody eyes!" And with that, Mandy stood up and left the kitchen without looking back.

After a few seconds, Claire heard the front door slam. "What's got her knickers in a twist?"

Claire had ignored Mandy's protestations about the signs being 'rubbish'. Mandy didn't understand her situation. She didn't understand how hard it was to be a lesbian and to never know for sure if the girls you're attracted to are interested.

It was easy for Mandy; she always had attention from guys, she was always getting asked out on dates, always being the one turning all the guys away. At first, way back when they were still in school, Claire had been jealous, she'd wanted to be the one asking Mandy out. But now she was starting to get used to the idea that at some point was going to have a boyfriend and she would have to be happy for her. Happy that Mandy was happy.

But right now, Claire had more important things to worry about. She had to confirm her suspicions about Jasmine.

It had been an interesting week, and she'd learnt a lot, but she was slowly building up a body of evidence which led her to believe: Jasmine might just be batting for the 'girl's only' team.

On Tuesday, she had worn a silver ring on her thumb. Totally definitely a sign she was gay.

Claire also noted that, although she never really wore men's clothes, she'd only worn a skirt once since Claire had moved in. But she did have a large collection of jeans and cords and at least two pairs of Doc Martens.

What she needed to do now was find out for sure, destroy all the niggling doubts, and put her mind to rest. So, she was, once again, scouring the internet in search of 'The Truth'.

Rather than looking up the signs of being gay, Claire was now dredging the strange world of 'getting a girl to like you'. She had found a crazy video that promised to give away foolproof tricks of seducing any girl, anytime, anywhere. A lot of this tutorial seemed to involve staring at a girl's lips and pretending to be popular. She had taken a few notes but to find out any more information she would have to take the full course, which was priced at $5,000, based in the U.S., and aimed at men. She decided to move away from that website.

Claire went back to her notes.

She had done more research and reading about 'finding the signs' than she had done on any of her courses. Her first few essays were due in just a few weeks. She knew she should be reading for them, but she just couldn't focus while she still had this hanging over her head. It was far too important.

There were a lot of indications that if a girl makes eye contact while talking, then she is interested. This seemed to directly contradict the whole 'staring at lips' tutorial she'd watched. She was going to have to try and see if she could stare at Jasmine's lips while trying to work out if Jasmine was making eye contact with her. That would be tricky.

She would also have to look for hair-flipping and arm-touching, these would be sure signs that Jasmine was flirting with her. But if Jasmine wasn't sure that Claire was gay then she may avoid flirting. So, Claire was going to have to be subtle about giving off her own signs.

Most websites had told her to mention celebrity lesbians and watch for a reaction. Claire didn't know of that many celebrity lesbians and although she now had a list, she didn't want to get into a conversation about any of them as she didn't know who most of them were. She would just have to talk about Ellen and Xena and see if Jasmine took the hint.

She was also struggling to find a local gay club (although she was sure that G.A.Y was one) that she could casually drop into the conversation. But even if she did, she felt that it would be a bit too obvious and she wanted to give signs that wouldn't be noticed by someone who wasn't also a lesbian, just in case things went bad. This needed to be subtle.

Claire looked at the long list of gay-friendly TV shows, the only one she had actually seen was Glee, and she didn't want to admit to that.

There were only really two options left.

The first was to ask if Jasmine was a lesbian and no way in hell was that gonna happen! But the second option was to get her drunk. Claire knew that it was a cheap night at the student union nearly every night, so she could try to casually ask if Jasmine was thinking of going out, then maybe meet her there, ply her with alcohol and see what happened. It was her best option by far.

She looked over at her phone.

Mandy still hadn't been in touch. It was well over a week now since she had stormed out. She missed her. But being gay was something Mandy would never understand so she would just have to accept that they were going to start drifting apart. Perhaps it was for the best; if she was still interested in Mandy, then her potential relationship with Jasmine could already be in jeopardy.

She grabbed her cup, wanting the last bit of tea but it was empty. It seemed such a long way down to the kitchen to get another one, but she was sick of looking at a computer screen.

'Besides,' she thought, 'I might run into Jasmine'.

As usual, she slowed down as she walked along the hallway passed Jasmine's door, she waited, hesitating. Trying to drag out the length of time she was there, just in case Jasmine walked out and she would have a legitimate reason to 'bump into her.' But after a few minutes, it was clear this wasn't going to happen and she slunk off down the rest of the stairs and headed towards the basement kitchen.

As she got closer she could hear voices, she didn't recognise them at first but then realised one of them was Jasmine.

She still hadn't met all the other housemates, so she was a little nervous as she stood outside the kitchen door. But she put on a smile and forced herself through, delighted to lay her eyes on Jasmine again.

But she didn't recognise the other girl, and she didn't seem to fit the description of any of the housemates.

"Heya!" said Jasmine, with a smile.

"Hey," Claire replied, trying to decide whether she should be making eye contact or looking at her lips. Jasmine's lips were beautiful, they were full and succulent, she didn't wear lipstick but she always wore lip gloss, making them even more irresistible.

"—from my course."

Claire only heard the end of the sentence, she realised that Jasmine had introduced the other girl but she didn't catch her name.

'Oh, crap,' she thought, 'Oh crap, crap, crap.'

"Hi," she said, taking the girl's hand. The girl seemed okay looking, a bit gangly, though. She was wearing a football shirt, and Claire tried to think of something to say about football, but she didn't know anything.

"What did you come here for? Am I in your way?" Asked Jasmine, trying to move out of the way of the oven, but not sure where to stand.

'What did I come here for?' thought Claire suddenly 'Why am I in the kitchen? What am I supposed to do?'

"My cup!" She said suddenly, waving her mug vaguely at Jasmine before stepping over to the sink to wash it.

'That wasn't weird,' she thought.

She slowly rinsed the cup under the running tap, not listening to the conversation going on behind her but wondering how she could drag out her visit, how she could stay in the kitchen with Jasmine a little longer. She couldn't cook, it was only an hour since she'd eaten, perhaps she could join in the conversation... she finished washing her cup and wondered how long she could convincingly drag out making a cup of tea.

"Ok well, see you later," the girl said, waving vaguely at Claire, before giving Jasmine a hug. Then she left and Claire was alone with Jasmine.

"So, what are your plans for the afternoon?" Jasmine asked, turning to her and smiling.

Claire tried to remember some of the things on the list, maybe she should say she liked football, only she didn't and that might cause problems if she was asked questions. She remembered the list of lesbian films, she should definitely go with that.

"I was going to watch something on my laptop, but I'm not sure I can decide which film to watch." She tried to think back to the list, all she could remember was 'Itty Bitty Titty Committee' and she didn't want to watch whatever that involved. But the words kept going around in her head: 'Itty Bitty Titty Committee,' 'Itty Bitty Titty Committee,' 'Itty Bitty Titty Committee,'—

"Star Trek," Claire said, suddenly remembering something about Sulu having a husband.

"I'm not really into sci-fi," said Jasmine.

"Neither am I." Claire had to admit.

"Oh. Well, Ali has just given me a DVD to watch, it's supposed to be really funny. If you want, you could watch it with me?"

'Oh, my God!' she thought. 'Oh, my God! A film! Watching a film with Jasmine!'

"Yeah, sure," she said coolly, trying to shield her excitement.

She tried to remember some of the signs to watch out for as she followed Jasmine up to her room. She thought about the arm touching, and asking her about lesbian bars, she wasn't sure what was the most important thing to focus on.

"Make yourself at home," Jasmine said, smiling and indicating the bed.

Claire made herself comfortable amongst the cushions

and pillows. She could smell Jasmine's perfume as she lay down, she tried to think about something else.

"What film is it?" Claire asked as she watched Jasmine place the DVD into her laptop.

"It's called 'But I'm a Cheerleader'."

"Oh," said Claire, disappointed. "Cool."

It sounded like a typical American teen drama, not really something she was interested in, but still, it would be great to watch it with Jasmine. She would have the next few hours alone with Jasmine, desperately hoping that somehow, she would find out if she was gay.

'OH. MY. GOD.'

Claire stared at the tiny computer screen, open-mouthed. She had no idea that this kind of thing happened in anything other than porn.

At the first indication that the main character might be a lesbian, she had been surprised, then at the mention of the gay camp, she had been intrigued. But as the film went on it became clear that it was something she had never encountered in her sheltered and untutored life; it was a lesbian romance.

When the main characters had started getting it on, Claire didn't know where to look! Yet she had been transfixed, feeling as though she shouldn't be looking but unable to resist, and confused about the etiquette of handling the situation. People aren't supposed to admit that they want to watch sex, so what do you do when your housemate shows you a film with sex in it? Where on earth do you look?

Thankfully for Claire the scene eventually ended, the

film returned to its former hilarity and she could bury her discomfort in slightly-too-enthusiastic-laughter.

She glanced across at Jasmine, giggling away, and wondered why she had chosen to watch 'But I'm a Cheerleader' with her. Claire was now almost certain that Jasmine was definitely a lesbian. The signs were there; the Doc Martins, the way she wore her hair, and now this film!

But 'almost certain' wasn't absolutely certain. There were still niggling doubts. What if she was just open-minded? What if it was just that a gay friend had lent her the film? But then what if Jasmine had purposely chosen the film to tell Claire that she was a lesbian!? To give out the signs loud and clear and now all Claire had to do was make a move...

'Oh GOD! How do I make a move?' she thought, desperately. She had no idea! 'Maybe I should lean closer?' She tried to, delicately, sidle up the bed, but all she managed to do was wobble the laptop, annoying Jasmine and making herself look like a beached dolphin flailing about on the sand.

Claire tried to think back to some of the advice she'd read online: bite your bottom lip, lick your lips, stare at her lips, all she could think of was lips, nothing else, nothing came to mind from those hours and hours of research! And for her to get Jasmine to notice her lips she would have to stick her head in front of the film and she didn't think that would go down particularly well. Whether she was managing to simultaneously bite, lick, and look, or not.

She suppressed a sigh of frustration and tried to focus on the movie, not really taking it in and doing nothing but thinking about Jasmine's lips. Maybe... just maybe... if she played her cards right, she would be able to do more than just think about those lips.

"So, what did you think?" Jasmine asked.

Claire hadn't even realised the film was over. "It was brilliant!" she said, a little too enthusiastically.

"I loved that bit with the guy trying to play football!" Jasmine said, laughing.

"Yeah! That was funny!" Claire sensed an opportunity; she knew she had a chance to take the conversation into an area where she could get absolute confirmation. Probably.

"So," she started, trying desperately to be casual but knowing her phrasing was going to have to be perfect to take this next conversation in the direction she wanted it to go, "I never knew they had those kinds of 'gay camps' in America," she looked up at Jasmine sitting regally on the bed, her legs kicked out to her side giving her the look of an Indian Princess, especially with her long dark hair and her deep dark eyes and those succulent, juicy lips. 'Focus' Claire told herself.

"Oh, yeah!" Jasmine started, clearly, she had some prior knowledge of this, which Claire hoped would play straight into her hands. "They still have some in parts, and not just in America either, there are a lot of people who think they can 'cure' people who are gay. In fact, it wasn't long ago that Boris Johnson banned a group of them from advertising on London buses, but I think he got into a bit of trouble about free speech."

"What do you think about all of that?"

"Free speech?"

"About the cures for being gay?" Claire asked, trying to keep the conversation on track. "Do you think people choose to be gay or can choose to stop?" she knew she would have to get a clear answer to that. She prayed for the right answer, she prayed that Jasmine would be open to the idea and then she could push her further on it.

"No, you don't choose who you fall in love with," Jasmine looked at Claire and smiled slightly, "If you love someone then you love them regardless, don't you?"

Claire felt every part of herself wobbling with excitement!

Jasmine had basically just admitted she likes girls, and that look! That look told Claire that she knew exactly what she was admitting to and was totally ready to open up about it.

Claire tried to speak, but her throat felt dry. "Yeah," she managed to say, she knew she had to ask her next question. Her skin was tingling with anticipation, her heart pounded in her chest and she struggled to keep her breathing on a steady level. She needed to sound calm and relaxed, she had to master this, to stay in control of the conversation.

"So..." she started. Unable to maintain eye contact with Jasmine, the nerves knotting in her stomach, "Is there anyone you're interested in at the moment?"

She had asked! There was no going back now, she'd committed to that conversation and in three seconds she was about to hear the 'yes' or 'no' that could define the rest of her life. Claire couldn't breathe.

Jasmine giggled.

Jasmine actually giggled! Claire looked up; she knew this was the moment. Her mouth was dry, her heart was going so fast she was almost worried it would explode.

"Actually, there, kind of, is someone... sort of," Jasmine said.

Claire wanted to scream. To shout and cheer and yell for joy, she couldn't suppress the grin that had spread across her face, but she had to keep calm. Had to stay cool and collected.

"Really," she asked, her voice slightly higher pitched

than it had been a few seconds before, "tell me more!" She was trying to go for the interested friend tone, but she thought she probably sounded more like a hysterical believer. But she knew she was close, so close! After all, Jasmine invited her into her bedroom, Jasmine showed her the lesbian film, Jasmine has been friendly to her ever since she arrived, and now Jasmine was acting all shy and coy as if she didn't really want to say anything and was being forced to open up, yet all this time she had no idea that Claire felt the same way! But of course, Claire wouldn't have to reveal anything until after Jasmine has admitted to how she felt... and that could be any second now.

"Well, it's a bit of a secret..." Jasmine whispered.

Claire thought she was going to have a meltdown, it was just too much, she couldn't take it. "Oh, you can tell me!" she squealed excitedly.

Then Jasmine looked her straight in the eye, they held one another's gaze while Jasmine seemed to be assessing her, trying to tell if this was the right moment.

'Tell me!' Claire screamed in her head.

"I'm in love with a girl."

And with those words, Claire thought she would die of exhilaration right then and there! She wanted to tell her she felt the same, she wanted to lean forward and kiss her, finally taste those sweet, juicy lips and let her hands run all over Jasmine's body.

She had been right all along! She knew from the very beginning, that moment way back when they first met, the very first instant; at that moment electricity had sparked and she had known the smile Jasmine had given meant something more.

She knew she was right to have done the research, and now it had all paid off! She was right about everything!

Jasmine was so totally gay and she had known! Her 'gaydar' had clearly worked brilliantly, she just had to have more faith in herself in future. She knew there was a spark between them, she knew that she couldn't have been alone in feeling that buzz of excitement deep in her belly when she looked into Jasmine's eyes. She knew secretly that Jasmine must have felt the same thing and now it was confirmed! Now, everything was justified! Sacrificing her first few university essays to get this moment right was totally worth it because now she could tell Jasmine exactly how she felt, explain how she had known from the beginning and she was just waiting for Jasmine to admit it.

She wanted to play one last card, she wanted to hear Jasmine say the words to her, she wanted to hear them on her lips and then she could kiss her.

Claire lay down on the bed, trying to appear as seductive as possible, without really knowing how to look seductive. She needed to be cool, calm and in control.

"Cool," she said, trying to sound husky, but the excitement in her voice meant she was still higher-pitched than usual, "anyone I know?" She asked but she knew what the answer was going to be.

She started to think about how their relationship would pan out, she'd be able to introduce this gorgeous girl to all her old friends, they would be so jealous of her. They certainly wouldn't laugh at her for being gay anymore, and Mandy would have to be so apologetic about how wrong she was to doubt any of this. They might even move in together, get some chic little pad somewhere and get out of this awful house.

"Actually, yes," Jasmine said.

Claire felt like the master of the conversation, completely in control of every step, every move that this exotic dance was taking. She smiled, knowing what was coming next, waiting in anticipation of Jasmine's admission of love, of her passion, of how she fell in love with her at first sight.

"Ali, the girl you met downstairs, and I have been seeing each other for about two months."

Claire's body seemed to stop working. She didn't understand, she heard the words, but she didn't understand. That girl? The gangly one? In the football shirt? But why? She wasn't even beautiful! She was nothing compared to Jasmine, she was sporty, she didn't wear make-up... why would Jasmine like her? When she had been so nice, so thoughtful, and when she had looked at Claire with that look?

"If her family finds out," Jasmine continued, "they will completely disown her, so we have to keep it a secret." Jasmine looked at her with those deep dark eyes of hers, so beautiful, so seductive, so interested in someone else, "I can trust you, can't I?"

As Claire's heart thundered to a crushing, juddering, smashing break, she smiled weakly and nodded. "Of course," she whispered.

SHE FELT PATHETIC.

She'd cried herself to sleep the night before. It wasn't just the rejection, it was how wrong she had been, how she had been so sure and yet set herself up for such a dramatic fall.

She felt stupid.

Claire looked at her pale and tired reflection in the

grimy bathroom mirror. She'd even moved into this hellhole because of her.

There were lectures this morning. Lectures she had to attend. Lectures that were starting in about twenty minutes. But Claire was still in her pyjamas and intended to stay that way.

She left the bathroom, not caring if she was seen in her make-up stained dressing gown, mismatching pyjamas and bunny slippers. There wasn't really any point in trying to make a good impression now. She was going to slob around the house, eating crap food and watching crap telly. She might even take up smoking for the day.

As she passed Jasmine's bedroom door, she remembered the moment from the night before, when Jasmine had announced her news in excited tones, when she had broken Claire's heart without a notion of what she was doing.

Claire heard giggling.

Two girls, giggling in Jasmine's room. Her heart sank as she realised she was going to have to share the house with Jasmine and her football-playing girlfriend all day. She couldn't do it. What if she bumped into them? What if they invited her in for a chat and a cup of tea? What if she heard more than just giggling?

She had to get out.

Claire ran up to her room and found clothes scattered about the floor, she didn't care what she was wearing, she had to get out. She had to leave. Within five minutes she was on the bus heading into Uni'. But she couldn't face a lecture.

In desperation, she looked at her phone and typed in the name of Mandy's new company in the City.

It had always confused Claire that the 'City' was actu-ally a small square mile inside London, which is itself a city.

So, it is a city in a city. She wondered if there was a pub or a club called 'The City' which she could go to, then she would be in 'The City' in the City, in the city.

It was only when she got off the bus on a busy street, drowned in tall buildings, where the sun could hardly reach, that she realised the City was not like the rest of London.

It was a soulless business district, with stern buildings and sterner people. Everyone wore black as if there was a national day of mourning and suddenly Claire felt very conspicuous in her bedroom floor outfit, which probably hadn't seen a washing matching since she moved to London.

There didn't seem to be any road names, and every street looked the same, it was a labyrinth of impossibility and Mandy was working somewhere inside of it.

Suddenly she wanted to cry. She felt lost. Like the time she had lost her mum in the department store. She'd hidden from the staff in the clothing racks as they had tried to catch the unattended child. She'd thought they were going to tell her off, it was only years later that she realised they had wanted to make her safe. It had felt like hours that she had been separated and alone. She had been terrified. Then when she finally found her mum, she hadn't even noticed that Claire had been missing. But she had found her mum. Even then, at four years old, she had managed.

Claire pulled herself together and looked at the map on her phone, she knew the offices were close. It was number 4-6 on this street. She just had to work out which way the numbers were running.

Only a few buildings had numbers on them, but she quickly worked out she was heading in the right direction.

Sixteen. Twelve. Eight.

This was it. A huge glass building with a security desk

and a couple of burly looking security men rather than the chirpy receptionist she had been hoping for. There was no way she would find Mandy in this maze of a building.

It was ten past twelve. She decided to take a risk and give her a call.

"Claire?"

"Mandy, are you free?"

"Yeah, I'm on lunch."

'Thank God,' Claire thought, "Can I meet you? I'm outside your building."

"So, you've finally come to take me for that congratulatory meal?" Mandy laughed.

Claire choked back the tears which were threatening to surface again. She had forgotten to congratulate Mandy, she hadn't even sent her a text about her new job. She was so obsessed over Jasmine she hadn't allowed herself the brain room to think of anything else. She was such a crap human being, "not exactly," she managed to say.

Mandy's tone changed. "I'll be right down." It was clear she heard the pain in Claire's voice and somehow that only added to Claire's guilt.

"You look terrible," Mandy said.

"Thanks," Claire replied, feeling utterly rubbish as she looked at Mandy in her gorgeous fitted suit: a pencil skirt, red heels, and a matching red top. She looked stunning, especially when compared to the monochrome of the rest of the City.

"I've only got forty minutes," she said, "But I know a little Malaysian place around the corner."

Any other day, Claire would have been thrilled. The exotic trip into the financial quarter, the secret quiet side street, leading into a wide-open square that seemed as if it was built to be hidden from tourists, and the quiet little restaurant with just a few suited and booted city folk, but not enough for it to be crowded. But today, her bed hair, unkempt appearance and her abject misery somehow took away the enjoyment of the experience.

"What do you want?" Mandy asked gently.

"I just needed to talk to you," she said, trying to prevent the tears from welling up, "I just feel so pathetic I had so a huge crush on Jasmine and I let it take over and I thought I had it so right and I had it so wrong, I'm such a crap lesbian, I've never even kissed a girl and I thought that I had a chance with Jasmine and out of all the people I've liked she's the first one that is actually a real lesbian and she's not interested because she's busy getting it on with some gangly, football fanatic who's completely unattractive and has no style whatsoever and blatantly does not deserve to be anywhere near Jasmine, who actually looks a lot like the real Jasmine, you know, the one in the Disney movie? I mean what has she got that I haven't?" Claire had to stop as she choked on her tears, and as they began to fall she picked up a napkin and started to wipe them away.

Mandy looked up the slightly startled waitress waiting to take the order. "We'll just have a seafood platter, then," she said, and the waitress nodded, relieved to be gone from the table.

"I'm just so pathetic!" she cried.

"You're not pathetic—"

"I was so sure, so certain! I should have listened to you. You knew right from the beginning what Jasmine was like and I just ignored you."

"I wasn't right," Mandy said, keeping her voice calm and steady to try to counteract Claire's whimpering, "I didn't know that Jasmine would have a girlfriend or even that she was gay... I just think that sometimes you can be a bit blind to the obvious, and maybe you should take things slowly and get to know people—"

"Oh! That won't get me anywhere!" Claire replied. She knew exactly what she was like, she knew that even now the too smart business people were looking sidelong at her, she knew she was obsessive and she was clearly stupid, "who could possibly like me after getting to know me?"

"Don't be mad, you're a wonderful person!" Mandy said, but Claire couldn't bring herself to agree, "you're caring and funny, you're sweet and you are really smart," Mandy didn't realise that her praise was only serving to make Claire feel worse about herself, "when you're not being dumb, that is," she added with a smile.

Claire looked away. It was hard to hear Mandy say those words, hard to hear such praise when she knew that Mandy didn't feel a thing for her. All it did was make her realise was how much she wanted Mandy, how much she had always wanted Mandy.

"You're bound to say that!" she said, trying to cover up her pain, "you're my best friend!"

"Yes, but that's why I am your best friend, you halfwit!" Mandy laughed, "I wouldn't be your best friend if all those things weren't true, can't you see what's right in front of you?"

Claire looked up at Mandy, she was so beautiful and so earnest. She had known that Mandy would try to make her feel better, but she should have known that Mandy would only ever make her feel worse. She shouldn't have come to see her. Mandy was the last person she should go to when she felt like this. When she has dressed in clothes she found on the floor and left the house without looking in the mirror, then she should not go and visit the beautifully styled Mandy. One heartbreak was now reminding her of another.

Claire knew then that the simple reason she had been so obsessive over Jasmine was to bury her feelings for Mandy, she was always trying to bury those feelings. Always trying to push them aside and find someone else to focus on. But whatever happened, she always came back to Mandy.

Perhaps that was the problem. If she was ever going to move on, she couldn't keep going back. She had to stop going back to Mandy, reminding herself of the pain. She should never have come here.

"I have to go," she said, suddenly, as the waitress brought over the seafood platter.

"What? Why?"

"I just can't..." Claire stood and left the restaurant; she couldn't bear it anymore. Perhaps in time, she would be able to explain to her why. But right now, she had to go, she had to be alone and find a way of moving on, making a clean slate.

"Claire!" Mandy had followed her into the street, but Claire kept her head down and kept walking. Mandy caught up and pulled her arm. "Claire, I want to help you!"

"You can't help me," and she knew it was true, she knew Mandy was just making everything worse. But as she looked at her with those beautiful eyes, trying so hard to help, it only made her angry, "you'll never..."

"Never what?"

Claire couldn't say it. But she wanted Mandy to feel her pain, to know how much it hurt just to look at her. "You'll never understand!"

"You still can't see what's right in front of you, can you?" Mandy said, grasping both of Claire's shoulders and looking straight at her. Claire didn't understand what Mandy was doing, and she wasn't in the mood for playing her games, "if anyone sees half of what I see they'll love you instantly."

Claire tutted and looked away, it almost made her laugh that Mandy didn't see the irony of what she was saying.

Then suddenly, Mandy kissed her. She pulled Claire forward into an embrace and pushed her lips against Claire's.

Claire was startled, frozen for a moment but then kissed back, feeling Mandy's soft lips against her own, holding her body close. After so many years of wanting her, she didn't care who walked passed, didn't care about anything else but that moment and holding the girl she loved.

"I love you," Mandy said, pulling out of the kiss, "you're dumb and stupid, your dress sense is bizarre, and you obsess over every girl you ever see." Mandy smiled and stroked her cheek. "But you're so brave," she said, "I could never have put up with what you did when you came out..." she looked away for a moment, "I so wanted to tell you how I felt, but I was so scared–am still so scared..."

Claire stared at her, stunned, unable to take in what was happening, unable to believe the words she was hearing, "but..." she said, thinking of all the times she had talked to Mandy, all the hours they had spent together, all the hours she had spent wanting Mandy, not knowing that she felt the same, "I had no idea" she said.

"I know!" Mandy laughed, but a tear had fallen across her cheek "I've been dropping hints for like, almost a decade!"

"I can't believe this is real." Claire didn't trust what was happening, after last night she didn't want to ever trust her senses again, "can... Can I kiss you?" she asked, hoping that Mandy wouldn't laugh at her, wouldn't walk away and say she got lost in the moment, it won't happen again. But she didn't walk away. She didn't say no. She smiled and nodded. And for the first time in her life, Claire took the initiative and kissed a girl. She took hold of Mandy's soft cheek, and gently leant forward, feeling Mandy's lips against her own. Taking the sweetness of her and feeling that now, maybe now after all this time she could be content.

"What do we do now?" she asked, still holding Mandy's cheek.

"Well, I think, probably the first thing we should do is go back and eat for our lunch!" They laughed, realising that the poor waitress must be wondering where on earth they had run off to; people normally eat and run, not order and run.

"And then what?" Claire said, hoping that Mandy wouldn't want to forget about this, that she wouldn't decide that it was too difficult and say they needed to 'cool off'.

"I don't know," Mandy said, "maybe we should just get used to being 'us' for a while."

"I think I'd like that."

And, hand in hand, they walked back to the restaurant and had their first meal as a couple.

THE END

RETREAT

She threw her cases on the bed and with that swift movement she felt as though she'd had something removed.

The weight of her stress was cast off and she threw back her arms and head, stretching and yawning, as the relief of solitude rushed through her.

'Alone at last!' she thought.

Then her phone rang. She sighed in resignation and grabbed it from her handbag.

"Grace." She said firmly, needing no other greeting.

"Oh! Miss... erm... er... Grace, I'm glad I caught you!"

It was her pointless new PA. She'd thought that a personal assistant was supposed to 'assist' her, not faff about like an inebriated chicken. But Pippa McLearny had, so far, proved her wrong on that count.

"Yes, Pippa?" She said, not bothering to mask her irritation.

"It's the 'plastics' order for the Grays presentation..."

"What about it?"

"They've just called to say they won't be able to deliver and the presentation is tomorrow..."

Grace breathed deeply, feeling the stress rising again.

"Right," she said, forcing herself back into business mode "plastics... What plastics exactly?

"For the presentation."

"Do you mean acetate?"

"Erm..."

Grace heard keyboard tapping, Pippa was clearly oblivious to exactly what it was that she was asking for help with.

"Yes! That's right it's acetate for the presentation tomorrow; 'creative' want to print out a number of their designs onto acetates to provide a more tangible experience to the client."

Grace sighed, exasperated. She had always worried that a team of creative people were unable to come up with a more creative name than 'creative' for their department.

"You'll just have to go out and buy some acetate." She said wearily.

"But that'll affect the costings!"

"Look, is there any way you can get the acetate delivered in time for the presentation?"

"No..."

"Do you have to have the acetate for the presentation?"

"Yes—"

"Then you will have to go out and buy acetate, even if it is four times the price."

"But—"

"NO!" Grace was sharper than she'd intended. "I don't want to hear it, Pippa. That's it. I'm switching my phone off."

She didn't listen to the protests. She held down the 'off'

button and watched the touch-screen disappear, then threw it on the bed with the rest of her detritus.

"No more." She said.

She wandered over to the french windows, where long muslin drapes hid the view. Pulling them back, she drank in her surroundings.

The health retreat was in a huge acreage of the country-side and from here she could see for miles. There was not a town, an office or even another building in sight. Just trees and grass and gardens and there, just beyond the cliff's edge, she could see the sparkling blue line of the sea, twinkling in the heavy sunlight.

Grace rested against the doorframe and closed her eyes, listening.

Nothing.

No traffic, no phones, no sirens, no shouting, no typing, no questions, no people. Just peace. And just below the silence, in a place she could never normally hear, there were the birds and even at this distance, she could hear the waves crashing against the rocks at the high tide.

'Just me' she thought. 'No one else. No one else is coming near me or speaking to me for a week.'

———

GRACE WANDERED DOWN TO THE RESTAURANT. SHE'D started getting restless in her room and wanted to try out some of the menu items she'd seen online. But as she stepped into the lobby, she noticed the restaurant was closed. She looked at her watch; four-thirty.

'Surely they should be open?' She thought.

She considered waiting in the bar but even for her it

was a bit early. Besides she had chosen this hotel for its grounds and solitude, so she ought to make use of them.

She turned and walked across the tiled lobby and out of the grand entrance into the gardens.

There was a warm haze on the air and although the sun was starting to cool, heat from the long summer's day was yet to fade, even with the soft breeze coming off the ocean.

She took a right and slowly headed along the path around the side of the hotel. There was no rush; she could afford to drift along the gravel path, run her hand through the tall plants running along the side of the hotel and stop to stare at a small fountain in the middle of a courtyard.

As she made her way towards the back of the hotel she saw that the gardens opened up to a huge lawn with a few scattered trees. She could see tennis courts on the far side and to the left, near a little copse of wood, was a walled garden.

Intrigued, Grace headed towards it.

A long fish-pond, strewn with lilies, ran down the middle surrounded by a flagstone path and perfect hedgerows. Statues of classical figures peeped out of the undergrowth as if they had been there since the fall of Troy. On the far side of the walled garden was a small mock-Grecian temple with a stone bench, perfectly placed to capture the afternoon sun.

Grace wandered over to it and sat down. She closed her eyes and basked in the warmth of the sun, listening to the distant waves and the occasional cooing of a wood pigeon.

She heard footsteps and opened her eyes momentarily, catching a glimpse of a woman in a long white dress, walking towards her. She was slow and graceful; her dress hugged her curves and for a moment Grace allowed herself to imagine that one of the statues of a Greek goddess had come to life. She closed her eyes again, dismissing the thought and enjoying the sun.

The footsteps slowly drew closer. But Grace determinedly ignored them trying to absorb herself in solitude and retreat from the world.

"Beautiful isn't it?"

Her inner self was screaming 'Me! Me! Me!' But she forced her eyes open, searching for the owner of the voice.

The woman was just a few feet away, her face was angled towards the sun with a soft smile on her lips, the sunlight gave her an ethereal glow, and sparkled on her auburn hair.

"Beautiful." Replied Grace.

She tore her gaze away, forcing herself not to stare and leaned back once more, closing her eyes.

The woman slowly drifted away without another word.

Grace couldn't help but open an eye to watch her leave, before silently admonishing herself.

'Strictly no flirting.'

THE SALMON HAD BEEN EXQUISITE AND THE GATEAUX divine, even with the raspberry coulis. She looked at the clock; it was six forty-five and still bright outside.

She'd brought a book and there was a television in her room as well as a huge bath, so she could spend the evening relaxing and then get an early night, but she had a restless energy that needed to be purged.

Her mind kept drifting over work matters; all the stress that had built up over the last, manic, six months. She needed to cleanse her mind and to be away from people. But when she pushed those thoughts away, the image of the woman in the garden replaced them; the way her body had moved as she walked down the path, the softness in her voice and the radiant glow of her skin.

Cleansing her mind was going to be difficult.

She decided to wander over to the bar and order a small red wine and finding a brochure, began leafing through it, occupying herself by planning out how she could work through every spa treatment that the hotel could offer and maybe every cocktail as well.

The barman placed her drink in front of her and on a whim, she asked if he had any ideas for how to spend the evening. He mentioned there was a wine-tasting class in the cellar. At first, she thought it a little odd that there was a wine-tasting course in a health retreat, but decided it was exactly the kind of event that would take her mind off everything.

———

THE CELLAR WAS DARK AND DUSTY: OLD LAMPS WERE hanging from the walls and gothic arches leading off down different corridors, all lined with wine racks. In the centre of the room were two circular tables surrounded by high backed chairs, giving off more of an impression of a séance rather than a wine-tasting class.

Grace sat in the only place that still had a free chair on both sides, but it didn't take long for someone to sit down next to her.

"Hello again."

She turned in surprise to see the woman from the gardens, smiling radiantly and she couldn't help but smile back.

"Hello!" She replied, convinced she must be blushing.

"I'm Alex." The woman said, holding out her hand.

Grace slid her hand into Alex's and her heartbeat slightly faster as their skin touched.

"Grace." She said, quickly withdrawing her hand and determinedly looking across the room as their host began to talk. She hoped that she would be able to ignore her attraction to this woman and focus on distracting herself.

Grace thought she knew her wines, but she'd never really sat down and compared them. She liked the first very much, but she felt the second may have had more 'body' to it, the third was delightfully fragrant and by the fourth, she'd learned the name of everyone on the table, had told the story of the time her brother lost a mattress on the A2 and had started flirting outrageously with Alex.

As the last of the wine was poured, people started to leave their seats and wander about the cellar, mingling with the other guests, complementing the course leader and purchasing their favourite wine of the night. But Grace and Alex remained at their table.

"You know, I think I may be more than a little drunk," Alex whispered.

Grace laughed.

"That could have something to do with the wine!"

Alex giggled before finishing off the rest of her drink.

"Shall we make a run for it before they persuade us to buy something?" She asked as she put down her empty glass. Grace looked at her, she knew she shouldn't, but she also felt that the offer of running away with Alex was too tempting to turn down.

They abandoned their table and sneaked past the other guests, running out into the abandoned lobby. Alex took hold of Grace's hand and led her up the main stairs onto the first floor, stopping outside one of the rooms and leaning against the wall.

"This is me." She said looking at Grace. "I've had fun this evening."

"Me too," whispered Grace, aware she was getting dangerously close to something complicated.

Suddenly Alex reached out and gently pulled Grace toward her and Grace didn't resist, allowing herself to be taken in Alex's arms. When Alex kissed her, she responded and before she knew what she was doing, her hands were running along Alex's waist and their bodies slowly bonded together.

A door slammed somewhere in the building, snapping Grace out of the moment.

She pulled away from Alex.

"I should go," she said, and, without looking back, she headed down the hall to her own room.

SHE WANDERED AIMLESSLY AROUND THE GARDENS.

At least that's what she told herself.

She told herself that she was merely going for a morning stroll to clear her head after a late night. But she quickly found herself back in the walled garden with the Greek statues. She took her place on the bench remembering the events of the night before. She felt so stupid, like a teenage girl with a crush.

That morning she'd already walked around the hotel, looking in the restaurant and the pool, wondering if she should sign up for a spa treatment, just in case she might 'accidentally' bump into Alex. Part of her was hoping that she would and yet another part was praying that she wouldn't. On the one hand, she felt as though she'd made a fool of herself the night before; leading Alex on and then running away. Yet she knew she had done the right thing.

Her life was so hectic at the moment. She'd been running herself ragged, working painfully long hours and never taking a day off. She knew that if she didn't take time away to just stop and clear her mind that she would run herself into the ground. Then when she did take a week to recuperate, she spent the whole time fawning over a woman she had just met and worrying herself stupid over a fleeting, drunken kiss. She wanted the world to just stop spinning so she could have a moment to catch her breath.

Eventually, she decided there was no point in wandering around hoping to catch sight of someone that she didn't want to see. Instead, she would go to the restaurant, order the next dish on her 'must-try' list and then spend the afternoon in the spa with her eyes closed and her face covered in avocado.

"MAY I JOIN YOU?"

Grace looked up; it was Alex.

She was wearing a little black dress and her auburn hair framed her delicate face. She smiled at Grace and then raised an eyebrow, clearly waiting for a response.

"Yes! Yes of course." Stammered Grace, unsure if she was terrified or delighted.

"Did you miss me?" asked Alex cheekily, as she took her seat.

Grace managed to laugh.

"It has been quite dull," she admitted.

As they waited for their orders to arrive, Alex chattered

about her morning. She'd been up the coast to a small fishing village for a look around and although Grace would have been exhausted by the expedition, Alex was clearly invigorated by it. Grace found herself energised by their conversation and the exuberance that seemed to ooze from Alex's very core. She was happy watching her talk, observing her movement and occasional flirtations, but there was still the nagging reluctance clawing at the back of her mind.

When dessert arrived, Alex was delighted by it and insisted that Grace try some of hers. She held the spoon out to her and Grace was helpless to resist. She leaned in closer and tasted the dark chocolate truffle.

"It's divine isn't it?" Alex whispered, and Grace couldn't deny that she agreed.

She found herself being led along by Alex and she wanted to take control back. She needed to be in charge and she needed to make this stop before it got out of control.

"I think," she said with a firm tone, looking directly at Alex "I'm going to head upstairs after lunch and spend the afternoon in my room."

"Well," said Alex with one eyebrow raised "I can't argue with that." Then suddenly she leaned closer "I think it's a marvellous idea."

Grace gasped as she felt Alex gently rest her hand on her thigh, the sudden, unexpected contact sending a rush of adrenaline through her. She knew then that she was losing control.

"In fact," whispered Alex, barely loud enough for Grace to hear, "I think I might go up to my room now."

Alex stood and left the restaurant.

Grace was stunned for a moment and simply watched her leave. She couldn't quite believe that Alex had taken her suggestion that way and wasn't sure if she should be flattered or concerned. She didn't need the strain of dealing with this situation and wondered if she should follow Alex and explain or whether that would make her look more of a fool, but then not going would be just as bad.

She massaged her temples. She didn't want to have to deal with this anxiety, she had come here to get away from stress.

Reluctantly, she realised she would have to follow Alex, she needed to explain. She left her table and hurried across the lobby, up the stairs, back to where they had kissed the night before. Alex was just unlocking her door. She looked up at Grace and smiled.

"Do you want to come in?" Alex's voice was low, just above a whisper and heavy with seduction. She held the door open slightly, looking at Grace, her little black dress clung to her body, begging to be ripped off. Grace forced herself to look away.

"Look, I'm not sure that this is such a good idea." Her body didn't agree, but she couldn't allow herself to be swallowed up by the moment.

"Must you always be the one in control?" Asked Alex, stepping closer. "Don't you ever just want to give up, run away from everything and let yourself go?"

Alex ran her fingers down the front of Grace's dress and looked straight into her eyes.

"I..."

"... to just stop thinking and worrying and to let someone else take the lead for a while."

"It's the middle of the afternoon..." Grace said, throwing out the only argument she had left.

Alex pushed open the door to her room and held out her hand. Grace felt that all her power to resist had been sapped away from her. Her ability to manage the situation and control others had abandoned her and she found herself placing her hand in Alex's and being led into her room. And as she gave in and allowed herself to lose control, she finally realised that was exactly what she needed.

THE END

MASK OF THE HIGHWAYWOMAN

T he carriage shuddered along the road. The sun had fallen some time ago and the passengers had turned to silhouettes in the moonlight. They were supposed to have arrived in Harrow in time for the four o'clock carriage to Bristol, but Evelyn was beyond worrying. She let her head rest against her seat, her eyes closed, as she concentrated on breathing, trying to keep her mind off the unsteady motion of the carriage.

Suddenly, the coach lurched backwards, Evelyn was thrown from her place as luggage rained down on the passengers, a woman screamed, and a child cried out.

"What's happened?"

"Is everyone alright?"

The child was crying as its mother scrabbled around the floor of the carriage. Evelyn picked herself up, she had fallen into the lap of the passenger opposite and she apologised as she tried to find her bearings in the dark.

"I'll go and speak to the coachman," said one of the men.

They could hear shouting outside, but before the

gentleman could reach for the handle, the door was wrenched open.

"Everyone out!" A masked man stood in the doorway; he was bathed in the light from the lanterns and held a pistol pointed towards the passenger's startled faces. They muttered between themselves as one by one they descended the carriage steps. The father of the crying child stopped to help his wife and then offered a hand to Evelyn.

"Come on, come on," the same voice called, herding the passengers to the edge of the lane. Evelyn looked back at the carriage, the driver sat with his hands held aloft and a man on horseback, similar in mask and dress to the first, held a musket aimed squarely at him. While another of the gang was searching the other coachman in the light of the stage-coach lantern.

"Everyone sit."

Evelyn turned in surprise to see yet another of the gang, at the edge of the road near the trees, pistol pointed at the six passengers and gesturing to the ground. Some of them began to sit down in the dirt, resigned to their fate. Despite the darkness, she could clearly make out the figure of a woman, masked though she was. She wore the same as the rest of her gang; boots, breeches, a long, fitted waistcoat, high-collared coat, and hat, and accessorised with a brace of pistols. The same outfit was popular with all highwaymen.

"I said sit," she repeated looking directly at Evelyn.

"I'd rather stand," she replied, "It's been a long journey."

"This isn't a picnic. I'm telling you to sit."

Evelyn held the woman's gaze a moment longer, before acquiescing.

"That was a stupid thing to do," her fellow passenger muttered to her as she sat down. He held his wife's hand as she rocked their child. Evelyn could see he was scared and nodded. She fully intended to keep quiet and allow the highwaymen to finish their task, without cause to harm anyone. She rubbed her arms to keep off the worst of the chill and shifted uncomfortably on the hard ground, listening to the whimpering of the babe, as the mother continued to rock, whispering to it softly. The gang had tied the coachmen together and were systematically ransacking the luggage as the passengers silently looked on. She allowed her gaze to drift towards the Highwaywoman, stood firm and resolute in her post watching the passengers, pistol raised.

"How much longer?" Evelyn asked. She heard the Gentleman quietly shushing her and so she rose from her place and moved towards the woman. "How much longer?" she repeated. The woman stared firmly back at her.

"Just sit down."

"I would simply like to know how much longer you intend to take. We are all cold and tired, the child especially. The journey took twice as long as it should have done! I am meant to be in Bristol by this time tomorrow and I have simply no way of getting there—"

"Then it doesn't matter how long we take, does it? Now sit down, or I'll make damn sure you never stand up again."

"That baby is freezing," she hissed, "it won't cope with much more of this." The woman's dark eyes left Evelyn's for a second as she glanced over at the mother. She then lowered her pistol and, with a flourish, removed her coat and placed it over the child, then raised her pistol once more.

"Now sit," she said.

"Thank you." Evelyn barely had time to touch the

ground before the gang had cleared the last of the luggage, and the musket-wielder stepped over to the passengers.

"One at a time," he said, scanning their faces "you first." He pointed his musket towards an elderly man, who rose clumsily and was immediately pulled into the middle of the lane where the light from the lantern spilt on the ground. He was searched, a purse pulled from his coat and a watch taken. He was then forced back into the carriage.

"You next."

One by one the passengers were relieved of their valuables and pushed back inside.

"How can you do this?" Evelyn asked the woman.

"Well, the pay is good," She said, smirking as she pushed Evelyn forward to be searched.

"Give up what you have, pretty one, or Johnny here will search you himself." The musket-wielder pointed to another man, he was taller than the others, and a heavy beard covered his face where his mask did not. Evelyn reluctantly fished her purse from her skirts, giving up all hope of finding her way to Bristol.

"And that," said Johnny, pointing to her necklace. Evelyn instinctively clasped her hand over it.

"No," she said, appalled at the idea of losing her locket.

"Hand it over," he said, stepping forward.

"No," she repeated, "it's of very little value, my shoes cost more."

"Well, I'll 'ave your shoes an' all if you don't hand it over." He reached forward to grab it from her neck and Evelyn stepped back into the arms of the woman, who grabbed her around the waist.

"Let her keep it," she said.

The two men looked at one another, the musket-wielder lowered his gun and looked back at the woman.

"No," he said, and struck Evelyn swiftly across the face with the back of his hand.

"Nothing is to be left behind,"

He wrenched the locket from her neck then shoved her unceremoniously back into the carriage, slamming the door behind her.

———

It had taken a while to get the carriage going once again. After the bandits had taken their leave, it had been up to the passengers to loosen the ropes on the coachmen and the horses had been startled into refusal for a while. But eventually, the saddened party had pulled into the Harrow coach house and Evelyn had arranged a bed, on the promise of a day's work on the morrow.

Tired, cold, and humiliated by the experience, Evelyn stood by the fire in her room and slowly undressed. They had left her trunk but, after going through it, she found that although her clothes remained, her jewellery and money were gone, even her pack of cards had been taken. She sat down in her nightgown and let the warmth slowly seep into her while she stared into the flames, contemplating her situation.

She heard a rattle behind her.

Swinging around, she stared at the window. The blackness beyond was empty but only for a moment. A face appeared, masked as the others had been. Evelyn gasped, standing up she searched the room for a weapon and drew the poker just in time for her attacker to throw open the window.

The cold air made the fire dance as the woman clambered, somewhat awkwardly, through the small frame and into the room before carefully sealing the window behind her.

Evelyn held the poker, raised and ready to strike as the woman took a cautious step forward.

"Don't come any closer," Evelyn warned, "you've taken everything I have, and if you touch anything else, I swear I'll—"

"I'm not here to take," said the woman, softly, raising her hand as she would to a spooked mare "I'm here to give back." She reached into her waistcoat and pulled out the locket. Still cautious, she held it up, and then placed it on the table near the window. "That's all I wanted to do," she said, backing off towards the window once again.

"No, wait!" Evelyn stepped forward, lowering the poker. "Why did you come here?"

The woman glanced back at the necklace, and then to Evelyn, her dark, brown eyes were soft in the firelight. "I could see how important it was to you."

"Thank you," said Evelyn, for the second time that evening.

"And you were right, it is worthless," she smiled, and again they stared at one another. "I should go," she said, "I'm sure there are search parties on the lookout for me this evening."

"Why did you do that?" Evelyn still held the poker firmly in her grasp.

"I told you, I could see how important it was to you."

Evelyn stepped forward and picked up the necklace.

"And I was sorry." Her hand drifted towards Evelyn's cheek. She winced as the woman stroked the bruised and tender flesh.

"I actually meant; why did you rob me in the first place?" The woman lowered her hand, "and scare those helpless people? That child could have died of the cold, and that poor mother..."

"Oh," she said, "that."

"Yes, that! As if it isn't hard enough getting by in this world, without people like you riding in and taking from those who can barely afford to get by—"

"That isn't true," she said, and Evelyn rounded on her.

"So, it wasn't you gallivanting in the woods with your band of merry men!"

"Keep it down!"

"Keep it down? Keep it down?! I have a good mind to hand you in myself," she shouted, "There is likely fifty pounds on your head, and I could do with the money!"

"You won't hand me in," said the woman.

"Won't I?"

"No. And I do not take from those who can't afford it. Only those who travel in the luxury of a stagecoach."

"You wouldn't call it 'luxury' if you had to travel in one."

The woman laughed. "Possibly not," she said, "but I am truly sorry that you were hurt."

"You've taken everything I have," said Evelyn, defeated, "and I have to be in Bristol by tomorrow."

"Yes. You mentioned that before. Why Bristol?"

"Does it matter?" Evelyn replaced the poker and turned back to the woman. "The fact is I cannot get there, and there is no-one in Harrow I can turn to for help."

The woman pulled a purse from her waistcoat, and dropped it, with a clunk, on the side table.

"I can't take that."

"Why not? It's your money."

Evelyn snatched up the purse, and counted the contents, before carefully replacing it in her trunk. "Who are you anyway?" she asked, turning back to the thief.

The Highwaywoman smiled, but shook her head, "I can't tell you."

"Why not? You trust me enough to come to my room late at night, you've rescued my locket, and paid for my journey, why can't I know your name? Or see your face, for that matter?"

The woman paused for a moment. Then, in the same flourish as before, she removed her coat, followed by her hat, and untied her mask. Evelyn stared. Her face was young, more of a girl than a woman. Her hair was dark and tied with a black ribbon, complementing the rest of her black outfit, she was tall, and her clothes were tailored, hugging at her waist.

"All is revealed," she said smiling.

"Not quite all."

The girl raised an eyebrow.

"I want your name?" Evelyn repeated.

"Oh... I really can't. I mean I shouldn't even be here I—"

"Give me your name or I shan't let you leave."

Evelyn wielded the poker once again, and the Highway-woman smiled.

"Then I should never speak again," she whispered.

Evelyn's stomach quivered, and it occurred to her that perhaps this girl felt the same inexorable pull that she did.

"I won't tell..."

"Bess," she said quietly, "call me Bess."

"Bess," said Evelyn, backing off from the girl and replacing the poker by the fire. She liked the name, it was both hard and soft, both child-like and regal. She sat on the bed, wondering how much more she could find out about the mysterious Bess.

Bess turned to stare into the fire, the soft light played on her skin, and her eyes shone with the flames. Evelyn made her way across to sit on the bed. She followed the line of the stranger's figure; her arms were strong beneath the light shirt and her fingers were long and elegant, softly placed on the arms of the chair, her waistcoat barely held in a shapely figure, and her breeches hugged at her thighs.

"Well this is all very strange," said Bess, pulling Evelyn out of her trance.

"What is?"

"I don't usually pay a visit to the people I have stopped on the road." She smiled, glancing briefly at Evelyn, half lying on the bed, propped up on her elbow and wearing nothing but her cotton nightshirt, before fixing her eyes back on the fire. Evelyn watched her slowly bite her bottom lip.

"Why did you come here tonight?"

"There was something about you," she said.

"What?" Bess pulled her gaze away from the flames for a moment and looked into Evelyn's soft blue eyes.

"I should go." She stood up and moved over to the table where her things lay, replacing her hat and coat while Evelyn watched, feeling a desperate need to stop her.

"Wait a moment," she said standing up to catch her as Bess reached for the window latch.

Bess looked back. "What is it?"

"Take this." She held out the locket, Bess looked at it for a moment.

"I can't take it. It's yours."

"Take it to remember me by."

"I don't need a locket to remember you," Bess said, placing her hand firmly over Evelyn's, holding on for just a moment, as they held each other's gaze.

Bess moved forward, just a fraction, before pulling back, but Evelyn reached out. She took the girl's cheek in her hand and guided her head forward until their lips met. Bess pulled Evelyn closer, grabbing her body with both hands. She could feel the soft flesh beneath the nightgown, the full length of their bodies pressed against each other, as they kissed, desperate and hungry. Bess ran her hands down the length of Evelyn's back but pulled away.

"I really should go," she said, unlocking the window. She climbed through and was gone in an instant.

Evelyn stepped forward and looked out in time to see a mounted figure riding into the darkness.

Slightly breathless, Evelyn closed the shutter and turned back into the room. She looked once again at the locket in her hand and then noticed, lying on the side table just as she had left it, the mask of the Highwaywoman.

THE CARRIAGE SHUDDERED ALONG THE ROAD, THE SUN had risen some time ago and light streamed in the windows, on to the passengers in the carriage. They had set out for Bristol at dawn and were making good time, but Evelyn was lost in thought. She stared out at the passing countryside which she had been so desperate to get away from. Thanks to Bess, she had been able to pay her lodging and get the first carriage out. But she was unable to shake off the thought that she shouldn't have left.

The coach lurched backwards, Evelyn was thrown from her seat as luggage rained down on the passengers, a woman screamed, and a man shouted out.

"What's happened?"

"Is everyone alright?"

'Not again' thought Evelyn as she picked herself up and

apologised, after falling into the lap of the passenger seated opposite.

"I'll go and speak to the coachman," said one of the passengers.

Evelyn could hear shouting outside, and before the gentleman could reach for the handle, the door was wrenched open.

"Get out!" A masked woman was at the foot of the steps, pistol in hand, one of the passengers stood to leave.

"Not you," said Bess, "You." She gestured toward Evelyn.

"I will not! Are you raving mad?" The passengers stared at Evelyn, surprised at her tone.

"I do believe I am. Now, step out of the carriage, or be damned to Bristol."

Evelyn paused for a moment as Bess reached a free hand towards her. She then grabbed her trunk from the floor and delicately stepped through the carnage and out into the early autumn sun.

THE END

ABOUT THE AUTHOR

Niamh Murphy is an author of adventure books with lesbian main characters. Her mission is to write exciting and engaging stories with women taking centre stage.

She is passionate about experimenting with different genres and has a fondness for romance, as well as action-adventure. She has written stories with vampires, were-wolves, elves, magic, knights, sorceresses, and witches as well as contemporary and humorous stories, but always with a lesbian protagonist and a romantic element to the tale.

Read more about her, and find exclusive free content, at AuthorNiamh.com

CPSIA information can be obtained
at www.ICGtesting.com
Printed in the USA
LVHW090407140121
676401LV00015B/1562

9 781520 984056